"Trust me, Rowena," he said softly.

A brave prince, she thought. Brave to take me on, and all the baggage I bring with me.

She looked down at their hands, feeling the strength of his seep into her veins. A helping hand, a loving hand, a hand she could hold on to. It wouldn't slip away from her, would it?

Trust me.

But could she trust herself to do right by him? She was no longer sure what *right* was. Only that Keir's hand felt right in hers. Was that enough on which to let the past go and forge a future together?

Dear Reader,

For many years my husband and I shared a
communication that crossed all barriers between us
and opened up doors we hadn't known existed. We
explored each other's private inner worlds in ways
that brought us much closer together. Frank became
more and more involved with the stories I was writing,
contributing ideas and slants I would never have
thought of myself. We enjoyed developing them
together, bouncing thoughts off each other, stretching
for the optimum result in whatever story we were
creating.

Frank suffered a stroke, then a heart attack
just before Christmas 1994. He passed away on
14 March 1995.

He wanted me to go on writing. So I sent my first
solo book to London. My editor loved it. She said
the hero was wonderful. I smiled. The hero is
everything my husband was to me. The book is called
Their Wedding Day, and you are just about to read it.

Do enjoy the book and think of Frank while you are
reading it.

Best wishes

Emma Darcy

EMMA DARCY

Their Wedding Day

Harlequin Books

TORONTO • NEW YORK • LONDON
AMSTERDAM • PARIS • SYDNEY • HAMBURG
STOCKHOLM • ATHENS • TOKYO • MILAN
MADRID • WARSAW • BUDAPEST • AUCKLAND

ISBN 0-373-11848-1

THEIR WEDDING DAY

First North American Publication 1996.

Copyright © 1996 by Emma Darcy.

This edition published by arrangement with Harlequin Books S.A.

® and TM are trademarks of the publisher. Trademarks indicated with ® are registered in the United States Patent and Trademark Office, the Canadian Trade Marks Office and in other countries.

Printed in U.S.A.

CHAPTER ONE

ROWENA couldn't let go without putting up a fight. A seven-year marriage didn't end overnight. There had to be some way to fix it, some way to stop what was happening. She had to see for herself this woman who had turned Phil's heart so cold to her and their children. She had to know what she was up against.

Despite the steady determination she had fostered from their home in Killarney Heights to Phil's work place at Chatswood, nerves fluttered sickeningly through Rowena's stomach as she drove into the basement car park of the Delahunty building. Her eyes quickly scanned the row of reserved spaces for staff. She didn't want Phil to be here. If someone told him she had come, he might try to prevent her from confronting the situation head on.

His red Mazda convertible was nowhere in sight. Rowena breathed a long, tremulous sigh of relief. As she manoeuvred the family Ford sedan into a parking bay, it suddenly slid through her mind that Phil might have lied to her about the flashy sports car being an impulse buy. Had he been re-imaging himself to impress the other woman? If so, what kind of love needed sexy status symbols?

Rowena wouldn't concede it was love, no matter what Phil said. This was another one of his flirtations, an ego boost that had somehow gone too far, probably pushed by the woman. Phil was a very attractive man. He earned a high income as Delahunty's chief property buyer. He was a catch in most women's eyes.

But she was his wife, and the flirtations had never meant anything before. A bit of fun. Phil had always assured her of that. Although it hadn't been fun for her, and it certainly wasn't fun now.

The shock announcement last night that he was leaving her for another woman, leaving her and their children and their home, had been so devastating she had barely been able to think, let alone try to change his decision. She hadn't even suspected their marriage was at risk.

It shouldn't be. Not when they had shared so much together, had so much together. Rowena would not accept what was happening. Not without a fight.

Some shallow infatuation... that was all it could be. Propinquity at the office. She had to believe that. She had to. Or seven years of her life lost their meaning.

She switched off the engine and checked her reflection in the driving mirror. Hours of weeping had robbed her green eyes of any sparkle, but at least the skilfully applied make-up concealed the shadows under them. Her eyelashes were long enough and thick enough to veil the slightly puffy lids.

The ruby-red lipstick looked rather stark against her pale skin but she had read in last Sunday's newspaper that vibrant shades were part of power dressing and gave a woman clout. Rowena was not about to appear wimpish to her rival. She might be a housewife but she was no walkover.

She brushed her fingers across the fringe that kept the thick curtain of her black hair from falling over her face. It needed a trim. Maybe she should have done something dramatic like getting her hair cut into a short-cropped style, make Phil take a second look at her, but he had always said he liked her hair long. The shoulder-length bob with the soft, razor-cut wisps that framed her face did suit her, and she had washed and blow-dried it to shiny perfection.

She fiddled with the red and green silk scarf she had tied around her neck to add some bold colour to her navy suit, then told herself she was dithering for no good reason and alighted from the car. She looked as good as she could in the circumstances. She hadn't let herself go. Her figure was slightly more rounded, more womanly than it had been before she had had children, but she certainly wasn't sloppy.

Whatever Phil had told his other woman about her, she was about to come face to face with the truth, Rowena thought, holding grimly to her purpose as she locked the car and turned to walk to the elevators. She checked her watch. Eleven-thirty. Time enough to say all she wanted to say before the lunch break.

A classy BMW swept into the car park and took the space beside the elevators. Rowena froze. It had to be Keir Delahunty, the one man whose path she least wanted to cross, especially today of all days!

It was difficult enough to come to terms with the fact that Keir was Phil's boss and always being mentioned when Phil talked about his work. She wished the job at Delahunty's had never come up. Or been won by some other applicant. Anything to be spared the connection to Keir and the memories he evoked.

No matter how better off they were financially from Phil's move to Delahunty's, it had been disastrous in every other sense, Rowena reflected miserably. First the unsettling effect of having Keir on the fringe of her life, and now this woman threatening her marriage. Having to face both of them was too much this morning. Better to go back to her car and wait until Keir had gone.

His car door opened, head and shoulders rising above the bonnet. There was no mistaking those broad shoulders and the thick dark hair. She started to turn away, feeling agitated at the loss of time, but more agitated at the thought of being caught with Keir Delahunty and having to share an elevator with him. Did he know what was going on between Phil and another one of his employees?

"Rowena..."

Her heart stopped. No avoiding him now. He'd seen and recognised her. He'd recognised her instantly at the company Christmas party a year ago, despite not having seen her since she was seventeen. Their association had been too long, too close—all her childhood and adolescent years—for him to forget her face. And, of course, there were other things that were unforgettable, however much one might want to block them out.

But she mustn't think about that now. She had to come up with some bright small chat to get her through the next few minutes. She took a deep breath to steady herself and turned to him with what she hoped was a surprised smile.

"Keir..." She forced her legs into resuming their walk towards the elevators. He remained by his car, clearly waiting for her and expecting some polite exchange between them. "How is everything going for you?" she asked.

"Fine! And you?"

She ignored that question in favour of concentrating on him. A brilliant architect and an astute property developer, Keir Delahunty had not let the grass grow under his feet over the last few years. While he'd established a highly reputable name on the northern side of Sydney Harbour, he was now spreading his business interests to other parts of the city.

"I loved your design for the town houses at Manly," she said with genuine admiration. "Phil showed me through them. They've all been sold already, haven't they?''

"Yes. They went quickly." He smiled, and in his eyes was the warm appreciation of a man who liked what he heard. It surprised her when he remarked, "You look very chic this morning."

"Thank you. It's kind of you to say so."

It was a boost to her confidence. If Keir Delahunty thought her attractive today, she had certainly covered up the ravages of last night's despair. Not that she welcomed such a personal comment from him. It was far too late, with far too much water under the bridge for her to want to be reminded of the attraction—the love on her side—that had been so cruelly severed eleven years ago.

He'd been handsome at twenty-four but he was even more impressive now, exuding the kind of effortless assurance and authority that came with a long line of successes in his chosen field. The terrible injuries he'd sustained in the accident that had killed her brother had left no lasting mark on him. He stood tall and strong and moved with the easy coordination of an athlete in top condition. Not for him the consequences that had torn her family apart.

Was he aware that she was facing a more immediate, more personal family break-up? Had Phil been indiscreet in pursuing this office affair? Why had Keir made a point of stopping to speak to her?

"I'm afraid you're in for a disappointment if you've come to see Phil. I left him to do a valuation of a warehouse at Pyrmont. He won't be back until well after lunch."

The information was welcome. "Thank you, but it's someone else I want to see," she said, her inner tension bringing a brittle tone to her voice.

Keir's deep brown eyes scanned hers sharply as she drew level with him. Had he sensed something wrong? She quickly moved towards the closest elevator, acutely conscious of him falling into step beside her. He pressed the up button. The doors slid open immediately, much to Rowena's relief. Another minute at most and she could escape from his disturbing interest.

A Christmas holly decoration was pinned to the back wall of the elevator. Christmas only ten days away. How could Phil leave her and the children at such an important family time? And the woman... She must be young and thoughtless and selfish to ask it of him. Or didn't she know about the children? She soon would, Rowena vowed.

"It's been a year since we last met," Keir remarked casually, gesturing for her to enter the compartment ahead of him. "I was looking forward to seeing you at the company Christmas party last Friday. Was there a problem with the children?"

A tide of heat swept up Rowena's neck and scorched her cheeks. Phil had lied to her about that, too, telling her the party was limited to staff only this year. She moved slowly to the rear of the elevator, hoping Keir hadn't noticed her embarrassment.

"I had another engagement," she said, instinctively covering up her husband's deception. It was too humiliating to admit. She didn't want to encourage any enquiries about the children, either. That was too close to all she had to contain.

"I wondered if you were avoiding me," Keir said quietly.

Such loaded words.

They pressed on Rowena's heart and constricted her chest. Why now? she railed desperately. She didn't need this on top of everything else she had to contend with. Pride forced her to swing around and face him as he followed her into the compartment.

"Why on earth should you think that?" she asked with what she hoped was credible astonishment.

His swift scrutiny was offset by a shrug. "Because of Brett's death. You could have ended up blaming me, as your parents did."

"You know I didn't. I visited you in hospital."

His eyes seemed to take on a piercing intensity. "Did you receive my letter, Rowena?"

She stared at him in confusion. Only days after Brett's funeral Keir had been flown to the United States for highly specialised corrective surgery, and that had been the end of any contact between them.

"When?" The word sounded like a croak from her throat.

"I wrote from the clinic in California. You didn't reply."

She shook her heard. "There was no letter."

He frowned. "I thought...assumed..."

"Well, it doesn't matter now, does it?" she cut in.

There was simply no point in a post-mortem over what might have been. Keir could have written again if she'd been really important to him. Or looked her up when he came home all repaired and fit to pick up his life. The past was gone. To open that sealed compartment and invite the old pain out into the open was more than she could handle. It was the present she had to deal with, and Keir was delaying her for no good purpose.

She forced a smile to mitigate any offence in the abrupt snub. "Would you press the button for reception, please?"

With a look of ironic resignation he turned to the control panel, lifted a finger, then unaccountably hesitated, passing over the button she had requested and pressing the one for Close Doors. He then faced her with a direct inquiry.

"Whom have you come to see, Rowena? I know all my employees and the departments in which they work. There's no need for you to stop at reception. I can direct you to the floor you want.''

It sounded friendly and helpful, but Rowena wished she could die on the spot. She wanted to say it was none of his business. The expression in his eyes told her it was his business. Everything that happened in this building was his business.

It was a bitterly capricious stroke of fate that her arrival in the car park had coincided with his. Here she was, trapped with him in a confined space, his eyes asking her for a direct reply. Even as she frantically sought some evasive explanation for her visit, the certainty came to her that he knew why she had come and what she meant to do.

Maybe the affair had been carried on so blatantly it was common knowledge throughout the whole building. Rowena inwardly cringed at the thought. Then pride clawed through the miserable weight of humiliation, pride and a fierce maternal need to fight for her children's emotional security. She had done nothing wrong. What other people thought did not matter when so much of real importance was at stake.

She aimed a direct appeal at the man who had the power to stop her. "I've come to talk to Adriana Leigh."

He held her gaze for several fraught moments, then slowly nodded. "Adriana works in an open floor area, Rowena," he said gently. "I'm sure you'd prefer complete privacy for your talk to her."

"I'm not exactly overwhelmed with choices," she confessed, her courage deflating at the idea of a public audience.

"May I suggest you use my office? I can call Adriana to come there, and I guarantee you'll both be left alone together to say whatever you wish to say."

Once again unruly heat burned into Rowena's cheeks. His sympathy to her plight was somehow shaming, yet to reject it was self-defeating. "Does everyone know?" The painful question slid off her tongue before she could clamp down on it.

"There's been gossip."

She closed her eyes, swallowed hard. "How long...how long has it been going on?"

"I don't know, Rowena." He paused, then quietly added, "More than three months."

Phil had bought the sports car three months ago. Last night's despair pressed in again. But she had come to try for a different outcome, to salvage what might not be a total wreckage. She had to try. She would try. She mentally constructed a protective shell around herself and opened her eyes. Keir was watching her, waiting for her decision, his expression carefully neutral.

"Your offer is...very kind," she said with as much dignity as she could muster. "Thank you. I'll take it."

He turned to the control panel. The elevator started to rise. Rowena fought to keep her com-

posure and her resolve. She watched the floor
numbers light up above the doors. They were
travelling to the top level of the building. Keir's
eyrie, Phil called it. She would soon find out why.

"Why are you doing this for me, Keir?"

It was an irrelevant question. Silly to ask it,
really. It put the situation on a personal footing,
which was the last thing she wanted to invite or
encourage with Keir Delahunty. Yet something
inside her had wormed past common sense...
perhaps a need for comfort from someone who
cared about her. Although Keir was probably
only thinking of saving his other employees on
the open floor area from what could be an ugly,
disruptive scene, causing more gossip and
stopping work.

He looked at her, his face grave, his dark eyes
intensely focused on hers. "We were friends for
a long time, Rowena. I remember it, even if you
don't want to."

Friends...and lovers at the end. Did he remember that? Or had concussion from the accident wiped out the memory of the night before
Brett was killed? She hadn't spoken of it when
she'd visited him in hospital. They'd both been
in shock over what had happened. She wondered
what had been in the letter she hadn't received.

She searched his eyes for some hint of knowledge of the intimacy they had once shared. It
didn't show. Maybe he had no recollection of it
at all. Maybe that was why he had never come
back to her. Maybe he simply remembered her

as Brett's younger sister, who had once had a schoolgirl crush on him.

The elevator stopped. The doors opened. He waited for her to exit first. Courtesy. Consideration. A friend. Brett's best friend all those years through school and university. Like another brother to her until... But she mustn't think about *until*. She had to think about Phil. And this imminent encounter with Adriana Leigh.

She forced her legs to move. She was extremely aware of Keir at her side as he directed her to his private office. A friend. She needed a friend. It was so hard...so very hard...to stand alone.

CHAPTER TWO

KEIR'S office was an architectural wonder in itself. The outside wall was constructed of massive glass panels, which were angled to extend over half the rooftop. The room was flooded with natural light.

At one end was Keir's workstation—desk, computers, library, several big drawing boards on stands made of round metal tube with hydraulic lift for height adjustment. Rowena was familiar with the latter. Her brother, Brett, had owned one. She remembered her father getting rid of it, getting rid of everything that connected Brett to Keir Delahunty, photographs, books, postcards, university lecture notes.

Then there was the burning of the sympathy cards and letters that so traumatised her mother. Had Keir's letter from California been burnt, too? It had been impossible to even mention his name in those dark months after Brett's death.

Tears blurred her eyes, and she quickly turned to look at the display of models featured on shelves running along the inner wall. These were the buildings Keir had designed, an impressive testament to what he had achieved by himself. It made Rowena wonder if his work took first place in his life and that was why he hadn't married.

18

Marriage didn't seem to be popular with high-powered career people. Easy-come, easy-go relationships probably suited their lifestyles better.

How different all their lives might have been if Brett had lived. He and Keir in the partnership they had planned, she and Keir... but that might not have happened anyway. Dreams didn't always come true.

At the opposite end to Keir's work area was a round table, furnished with contoured leather armchairs set on swivel bases. He ushered her to one of these seats, then excused himself to speak to his secretary, whose office they had bypassed.

Rowena was glad of the opportunity to sit down and reconcentrate her mind on the problem of Adriana Leigh. Yet it was difficult to come to grips with the idea of a woman she had never met, never seen. *I'll know more when she walks into this room,* Rowena assured herself, trusting instinct more than unsubstantiated guesses.

Her gaze drifted to the window view on the other side of the table. It was nothing dramatic, just blocks of homes on tree-lined streets stretching out over the suburb of Chatswood, streams of cars taking people to their chosen destinations, everyday lives going on as they invariably did, regardless of death, births, marriages.

And divorces.

Would it come to that for her?

An underlying sense of panic started churning through her stomach again. She didn't want to bring up three children alone. She remembered how hard it had been without a helpmate when Jamie was little. Phil had been so kind and generous, taking them both into his heart and life.

She had tried to be the best of all possible wives to him, although in her heart of hearts she had known she didn't feel for Phil what she had once felt for Keir. It was a different kind of love, less passionate, almost motherly in some ways. Despite being five years older than her, Phil could be boyish at times, wanting to show off, to be the centre of attention.

Looking back over the past year, Rowena had to acknowledge their marriage had become rather flat and routine. But surely every relationship had its highs and lows. It was a matter of working at it, being committed, trying to make it as good as it could be. Both parties were responsible for that. She didn't understand why this was happening to her. What had she done that was so wrong?

The sound of the office door opening snapped her mind to the immediate present. Keir returning, having summoned the woman she would soon be facing. He looked so big and powerful, a rock to lean on, and Rowena ached for the support that his caring seemed to offer, yet she knew she couldn't afford to let Keir close to her. It could only muddle everything far more than it was already muddled.

Keir didn't know he had left her pregnant eleven years ago. He knew nothing of the son she had given birth to nine months after the fatal accident that had destroyed so much. She had come to believe he didn't want to know, long before she had married Phil.

Whether that was true or not, it was not possible to change the course of events that had taken place. Phil had legally adopted Jamie. To all intents and purposes, Phil was Jamie's father. It was best for everyone if it stayed that way.

Nevertheless, Rowena allowed herself the indulgence of really studying Keir for the few seconds it took him to walk down the room, noting the likenesses to her son... *his* son.

Deeply socketed eyes, although Jamie's irises were hazel, a mixture of her green and Keir's brown. The hairline was strikingly similar with a cowlick at the left temple. Jamie's upper lip was softer, fuller, more like hers, and the shape of his face was rounder, less hard-boned. Perhaps as Jamie got older, his jawline would firm into the same mould as Keir's, but that was not obvious yet.

Her gaze skated down the perfectly tailored grey business suit to the stylish leather shoes on Keir's feet, feet she knew had longer second toes than the big ones. The mark of a fast runner, Keir had laughingly told her. Jamie had them, too, and he was the best sprinter in his age group at school.

"Rowena..."

She sighed and lifted her gaze.

"Would you like coffee brought in?"

She shook her head.

"Is there anything else I can do for you?"

"No. I'm grateful to you for this chance to get things straightened out, Keir. This is all I want. I won't be making a nuisance of myself."

"I'd never consider you a nuisance, Rowena," he said seriously.

"You know what I mean." She grimaced. "I don't intend to subject Delahunty's to a series of hysterical scenes."

"If I can be of any service to you, at any time, please call me, Rowena. I'll do all I can for you," he assured her.

She could see the deep sincerity in his eyes, and it hurt. Unbearably. *Where were you when I needed you?* she cried in silent anguish. *It's too late now. Our lives have moved on.*

A courtesy knock on the door heralded its opening. Rowena shot to her feet and stepped away from the table, inadvertently moving close to Keir, who merely turned to greet the new-comer. She wasn't seeking his support or protection, and wasn't aware of how they looked together as Adriana Leigh entered the office.

"Good morning, Mr. Delahunty," she said with a bright, winning smile. Her elegance, sophistication and complete self-assurance were heart-joltingly evident. Not a younger woman. Very much a woman of considerable worldly experience. Rowena was spared a flick of curiosity, but the full beam of Adriana Leigh's concentration was on Keir as she added, "What can I do for you?"

She was the kind of woman who was always aware of men and knowingly watched for her impact on them. Rowena recognised that instantly. She also knew instinctively there would be no tapping any vein of sympathy or guilt. In a roomful of women, this woman would be bored.

"I'd be obliged if you'd give some time to Mrs. Goodman, Adriana," Keir answered, his clipped tone making the request more of an order. "Rowena, this is Adriana Leigh."

The bright smile was only briefly jolted. She batted her eyelashes at Rowena. "How do you do, Mrs. Goodman?" A honeyed voice, dripping with confidence. With barely a pause, she inquired, "Did Phil ask you to come?"

It was a bold and subtle sliding in of the knife.

"No. It was my decision," Rowena replied, silently challenging the other woman to make something belittling of that.

Adriana Leigh raised perfectly arched eyebrows at Keir. "This is rather different from the usual bounds of work requirements, Mr. Delahunty," she pointed out, maintaining her decorum while questioning the propriety of his authority in what they all knew to be a personal matter.

"Sometimes extraordinary situations arise," Keir answered smoothly. "I understood your position as personal secretary to one of my executives requires an ability to handle delicate matters with courtesy and patience." He paused.

Was there a threat left hanging? "However, if you feel unable..."

"Not at all, Mr. Delahunty. As you say, I am used to dealing with such situations."

"I thought you would be." A touch of dry irony.

"I'll do my best to give Mrs. Goodman satisfaction," she said with her own touch of irony as she started forward, showing no further reluctance to join them by the table. A smart, intelligent career woman would do no less after Keir had put her skills in question.

Rowena concentrated on assessing everything about Adriana Leigh before they were left alone together. She had long, toffee-coloured hair, liberally streaked with blonde and deliberately styled in a casually tousled look. It was not only suggestive of a recent tumble in bed but a ready receptiveness to repeating the pleasure at any time.

She wore a long-sleeved, transparent cream blouse with a lace-trimmed, silk camisole underneath. Her full breasts jiggled freely. Her hips swayed, their voluptuous curve from a small waist emphatically outlined by a tan gaberdine figure-hugging skirt that was buttoned down to thigh level and left free to swing from a side split. She wore high heels. High, high heels.

This woman exuded sexuality, flaunted it, and Rowena doubted any man would be a hundred percent proof against it. There was no problem in understanding the attraction for Phil. The question was how deeply did Adriana Leigh have her claws into him?

"Rowena." Keir took her hand, pressing it to pull her attention to him. "I'll be in my secretary's office. You have only to call me."

Part of Rowena's mind registered his earnest concern and caring. She felt the warmth and strength of his touch. She had a craven urge to cling to it, but the purpose that had brought her here made it inappropriate. Badly inappropriate. Didn't he realise that?

"I'm all right, Keir. Thank you," she said in deliberate dismissal.

He gently squeezed her hand before letting it go. Adriana noticed it. Her amber eyes gleamed feline derision at Rowena before she turned her gaze to watch Keir make his departure. The moment the door was closed behind him, she opened hostilities.

"How did you come to be so cosy with our Mr. Delahunty?"

Rowena ignored the dig. "Do you love my husband, or is he simply another conquest to you?" she asked with quiet dignity.

It won a flicker of surprise. "Well, you're certainly direct."

"I'd appreciate a direct answer."

Adriana led from the chin. "I love Phil and he loves me and there's nothing you can do about it."

"You must have known he was married."

"So what? *He* knew he was married, too. I didn't take anything from you. You'd already lost it. Phil came to me." Gloating triumph. Power. No sense of guilt whatsoever.

"Are you married?"

"No."

"Divorced?" Perfect and obviously expensive make-up gave Adriana Leigh's face a youthful glow, but Rowena had no doubt this woman was in her thirties, possibly older than Phil, who was thirty-three.

"No." She was amused by the questioning.

"Children?"

Her laughter was mocking. "Two abortions." There was a hardness in her eyes as she added, "I won't go down that road again."

It made Rowena wonder if previous lovers had let Adriana down, and she felt a twinge of sympathy, remembering the pain of being left without Keir's support when she was pregnant with Jamie. The sympathy was short-lived. There was none coming from Adriana for the situation Rowena faced.

"Has Phil ever mentioned our children?"

She shrugged. "Emily is five and Sarah is three. They're young enough to get over the separation without any lasting trauma. The boy is old enough to look after himself. It's not as though their father has played a great role in their lives."

"Is that what Phil told you or what you want to assume?"

"I know the hours Phil works," she said smugly.

"Since *you* entered his life." That truth was obvious now. Rowena silently castigated herself for not realising Phil's long hours and overnight trips could have another purpose besides work. How complacent she had been to attribute it to ambition!

"Doesn't his desire to stay with me tell you something?" Adriana taunted.

Rowena hated her mocking amusement. She might be guilty of complacency, but she hadn't gone out hunting another woman's husband to fill in the lonely hours. It took all her willpower to keep her voice steady, her demeanour unruffled. She would not give her antagonist the satisfaction of goading her out of control.

"I suppose you think you've rearranged his priorities. For the short term," Rowena emphasised, wanting to shake Adriana Leigh's complacency. "Passion does tend to burn out."

"You don't know much about men, do you?" Pitying condescension. "They have two brains. Keep the one below the belt satisfied and you can bend the other any way you like."

Such heartless calculation sickened Rowena. Phil preferred *this* woman to her? "If that's the case, I find it odd that you haven't been able to hold onto one of the many men you've obviously had in the past," she retaliated.

"I haven't wanted to until now."

"Then your theory hasn't exactly been tested, has it?" Rowena pointed out, to no effect whatsoever.

"Face it, darling, you're beaten. You've never satisfied Phil as I do. That's a fact." The cat's eyes glittered down Rowena's classic navy suit and up again. "I daresay you're too much of a lady."

"There's more to a relationship than sex," Rowena declared with conviction.

"What?"

"Companionship, sharing goals and achievements, caring about each other, understanding..."

Adriana laughed. "Tell that to a sex-starved man. And there's so many of them around. Especially fathers."

The unexpected singling out of fathers bewildered Rowena. She stood, speechless, as enlightenment came in a shower of scorn.

"You dedicated mothers tend to focus all your energy on your children. Your attention is divided. You get tired. You have headaches. And the door opens for another woman to give a man back what his children have taken from him. Quite suddenly he doesn't give a damn about his children any more. He wants a woman in his life, not a mother."

"I'm sure that's what you'd like to think," Rowena said tersely, disturbed by Adriana's knowingness. Had Phil complained to her that his wife ignored his needs?

"I'm giving you some good advice for the next time around. The world is full of discontented married men."

"Why pick on Phil?"

"He was here. He's what I want. I'll keep him happy."

Rowena dearly wanted to rattle Adriana's mind-battering confidence. A flash of intuition came to her. "Phil wasn't your first choice, though, was he?"

A pause. A flicker of wariness. Then a return to aggression. "He's my last choice, and I'll make it stick, so don't think you can muddy the issue."

Rowena pressed further. "You got a job here so you could be around Keir Delahunty and try to catch his interest. He's the bigger prize, isn't he? Only he didn't take the bait."

Her eyes narrowed with anger. "Did he tell you that?"

"You were still flashing availability signals at him when you came into this office. You'd drop Phil if Keir gave you any encouragement."

Adriana snorted. "That man is made of stone. Phil's much more my style, and he knows it. You can't put Keir Delahunty between us."

That was probably true, Rowena thought in painful frustration. It didn't matter how right her observation was about Adriana's motivations, Keir obviously had a fine sense of discrimination in judging women on the make and wasn't interested. Why on earth couldn't Phil see... But maybe Adriana was right about him feeling neglected, overlooked in favour of the children's needs.

What was the best balance for being both a wife and mother? And why was the onus on her? Shouldn't a good marriage be mutually supportive?

Her head spun between a confused sense of guilt and a sickening sense of having all her ideals betrayed. Coming here, speaking to this woman, was worse than futile. There was no help in it. None at all. If Phil wanted Adriana Leigh, then let him have her, she thought, resolution undermined by a tidal wave of deep hurt and disillusionment.

But what about the children?

"I take it you're not overly keen about the role of stepmother," she said flatly, trying to think of anything that might change the situation, might give Adriana pause for second thoughts about a future with Phil.

"You chose to have kids. They're your responsibility. Not mine."

"You honestly believe Phil will be happy about shutting them out of his life?"

"Put it this way. You needn't worry about any fight over custody. Phil may want to see the girls now and then, and I'll be happy to go along with that."

"You're forgetting Jamie."

Again she shrugged, as though the burden was not hers to shoulder. "Well, he's not really Phil's, is he?" she drawled meaningfully.

"Phil is the only father Jamie's known."

"Whose fault is that?"

Angry heat crept into Rowena's voice despite her resolution to keep cool. "Phil adopted Jamie as his son."

"When he was how old? Four?"

"Three."

"No difference. He was a little boy, not a baby. The feeling's not the same no matter how you want to dress it up. The boy is yours, not Phil's, and at his age, he's bound to be a sulky troublemaker."

Rowena could not trust herself to suppress her outrage at these callous sentiments. Her body was beginning to tremble. "Thank you," she said tightly. "I won't take up any more of your time."

"Thank you," Adriana returned snidely. "It's always interesting to meet the wife."

CHAPTER THREE

"MRS. GOODMAN has said all she wishes to say to me, Mr. Delahunty."

Adriana's light, almost flippant tone made Keir grit his teeth against an unwise snap. It would be unprofessional to reveal the strong antipathy he felt, knowing as he did that it was aroused by his sympathy for Rowena. He had no right to any personal involvement with this affair. It behove him to maintain some objectivity.

He unhitched himself from the edge of his secretary's desk in deliberate slow motion. The report he'd been trying to read was still in his hands, and he used it as a point of dismissal. "Thank you for your cooperation, Adriana."

"My pleasure."

"To give pain?" The biting, judgmental words were out before he could monitor them. At least he had the satisfaction of wiping the smug look off her face.

"I didn't ask for this meeting, Mr. Delahunty," she coolly reminded him.

"A matter of opinion, Adriana. It's my experience that changing people's lives incites retaliation, even when the change is innocently caused."

Rowena's parents had taught him that. Not that this self-obsessed woman would care what damage she wreaked in going after what she wanted. They were empty words to her.

"I don't want more company time wasted on gossip, Adriana," he went on, chilling her out of any further comment. "I'd advise you to keep your meeting with Mrs. Goodman entirely private. Do I make myself clear?"

"Perfectly, Mr. Delahunty. I appreciate your tact."

He nodded.

She left.

He turned to his homely, middle-aged secretary. "Same for you, Fay. No talk about this."

"Locked box," she replied, giving him her owl look.

The tense muscles in his face relaxed into a smile. He liked Fay Pendleton. She not only delivered everything he asked of her with a minimum of fuss and maximum efficiency, her wonderfully expressive face and dry sense of humour always amused him. As did her hair, which was burgundy with wide, blonde streaks at the moment. Every three months she experimented with a new colour combination. Grey, she had declared, was too dull for her.

"I'll check this later," he said, dropping the report she had prepared for him on her desk. "Would you make some coffee, Fay, and bring it in with the sandwiches as soon as they're delivered?"

"Will do."

He wasn't about to let Rowena go without any sustenance. She had probably been too wrought up to eat breakfast, and Adriana had undoubtedly gone for the kill. Rowena would be in no fit state to drive. She shouldn't be alone, either.

Keir reached the office door in a few quick strides. He didn't know if Rowena would welcome his company or not. He remembered the polite barrier she had maintained between them at last year's staff Christmas party. He had felt then that she wanted no part of him, and he had reluctantly respected her wishes. It was probably only the shattering effect of knowing her marriage was on the rocks that had allowed the old sense of familiarity to break through this morning. He hoped....

Well, he could only try.

As he entered the office and closed the door quietly behind him, he was intensely aware of the need to tread very carefully. Rowena had come to do what she could to save her marriage. She wanted—loved—Phil Goodman. She was not looking for another man in her life, certainly not in any close capacity.

She sat with her elbows on the table, her head in her hands, fingers pressed tightly to her temples. Pain, defeat...and there was nothing he could do about either. It flitted through his mind that Brett would have pummelled Phil Goodman, inflicting hurt for hurt to his little sister. Keir knew it would do no good in these circumstances, yet he found himself empathising with the urge to do violence. Rowena deserved to be valued. To be cast aside for a woman like Adriana Leigh...

Keir took a deep breath, unclenched his hands and headed down the room to offer what comfort he could. Maybe she would accept a shoulder to cry on. Maybe she would let him drive her home. Maybe there would come some time in the future when she could view him as a friend again. More than a friend.

He was acutely conscious of the hole in his life, the emptiness that no one had been able to fill since Rowena and Brett had been lost to him. A bond of long sharing and understanding had been broken, and the years since had only hammered home how precious and rare it had been. It was impossible to get Brett back, but Rowena...

Dared he lift her from that chair and enfold her in his arms?

She looked up.

Her beautiful green eyes were awash with tears.

There was no decision-making.

He simply did it.

CHAPTER FOUR

IT HAPPENED so fast, Rowena was scooped from the chair and wrapped in Keir Delahunty's embrace before she could even begin to think it was wrong to have such intimate contact with him. Then the impact of his body against hers threw her into confusion.

She wasn't used to being held closely by any man but Phil. It had been so long since Keir had made love to her, yet she was instantly reminded of how it had felt with him. It made her acutely aware of both her sexuality and his.

Images of their youthful nakedness flashed into her mind. Her breasts, pressed flat to his broad chest, started prickling with disturbing sensitivity. Her thighs trembled with the shock of recognising the virile strength of his. Her back burned under the cocooning warmth of his arms. All normal thought processes were paralysed by sensations she was utterly powerless to stop.

One hand slid up to her neck, his fingers splaying through her hair as he gently pressed her head onto his shoulder. Her heart seemed to pound in her ears. The scent of some tangy aftershave lotion assaulted her nostrils. Her stomach contracted in sheer panic at the memories evoked.

"You don't have to fight the tears, Rowena," Keir murmured, his cheek resting against her head. "You can let out the grief with me. Just as you would with Brett if he were here."

Guilt that she no longer had a big brother? Sympathy for her pain? The tears were gone, shocked back to the well of despair that Keir's action had suddenly submerged. She shouldn't be feeling other things, but she was. And it was wrong. Terribly wrong!

Her mind shifted from one turmoil to another. Was Keir remembering other times when he'd held her, not as a surrogate brother but as a man who wanted her, needed her to be a woman with him?

She was not seventeen any more. She was well and truly a woman, an experienced woman who was in a highly vulnerable state, with her marriage on the rocks and her husband in love—or lust—with someone else. Did Keir think that made her available to him?

Why hadn't he married? What kind of man was he now? She didn't know. The meeting with Adriana had left her feeling she was a naive fool who didn't know anything!

It was as though all the foundations of her life had been ripped away. Was Keir a steady rock that she could cling to? Confide in? Or was there danger in trusting him, danger in trusting anybody?

His cheek moved, rubbing over her hair. His mouth—surely that was his mouth—pressing warmth...kisses! Her heart kicked in alarm. She jerked her head back and looked up. It wasn't brotherliness she saw in Keir's eyes. There was no soft sympathy. She caught a darkly simmering passion that triggered a tumultuous eruption of the doubts and fears Adriana had raised.

"Let me go!" she cried, pushing herself free of his embrace as he loosened it.

"Rowena..."

The gruff appeal fell on closed ears. Her eyes flared a fierce and frightened rejection as she backed away from his trailing touch. "Adriana's right. Sex is all that matters with men."

"No," he denied strongly.

But Rowena took refuge in walking over to the glass wall beyond the table, putting a cold, safe distance between them, wrapping her arms around herself, hugging in the pain of hopeless disillusionment.

She was a married woman. It was wrong of Keir to pretend to offer brotherly comfort and then use the opportunity to change it to something else. Even though Phil... But that didn't excuse it. Keir must realise she had come to save her marriage if she could. For him to take advantage of her weakness at such a time placed him on the same moral level as Adriana Leigh.

"*She* would have had you." The words burst from her, the bitter irony of his behaviour being similar to Adriana's striking her hard. "Why didn't you take her on, Keir? She was handy, available..."

"Rowena, I care about you. I always have."

The soft answer stirred more turmoil. She clutched wildly at the first reason she could think of to disbelieve him. "Then why didn't you stop what was happening between Adriana and Phil?"

No answer.

She swung around to probe further. "Don't tell me you didn't know she fancied you, Keir. Even I saw the signals when she walked into this room."

His face tightened as though she had hit him, yet there was no backward step in the dark blaze of his eyes. "You want a husband that needs to be rescued from another woman?" he challenged, a sting of contempt in his voice. "Face it, Rowena. Phil isn't worthy of your love. If he really cared for you, Adriana wouldn't have had a chance with him."

Phil *had* cared for her. Rowena was not about to forget he had cared when Keir's so-called caring wasn't anywhere in touching distance. "Who are you to judge that? Maybe it's my fault. Maybe I didn't give him enough...enough—"

"Sex?"

Heat flooded up her neck and scorched her cheeks. It was too shaming to concede she must have left Phil dissatisfied in that area, yet it had to be true. She bit her lips, wishing she hadn't started this tasteless argument. Even Keir's mouth was curling in disgust.

"Sex isn't the glue that keeps a man and woman together, Rowena. It helps, but if other things are missing..." He paused, compelling her full attention. "You have so many desirable qualities, any man should consider himself fortunate to have you in his life."

Desirable. Is that how Keir saw her? Still? But he had no right. And she mustn't let herself get confused and distracted.

"The evidence is against it," she reminded him. "Phil wants to be with Adriana. Everything we've shared means nothing against what she gives him."

"She strokes his ego, Rowena," he said flatly. "Phil likes to be stroked. He can't have enough of it. He never will have enough of it. Surely you've recognised that weakness over the years."

"Then why did you hire him?" she demanded, trying to reject his clear-sightedness about Phil's vulnerability to flattery. It went against her ingrained sense of loyalty to accept it.

"He's good at his job."

"Why did you hire her?"

"I didn't. Phil did. He's entitled to choose the staff that work with him. Usually it makes for a more effective team."

All perfectly reasonable. Rowena was left floundering in a quagmire of emotions with no outlet for them. A knock on the office door provided a welcome distraction.

A woman entered, pushing a traymobile. Either the silence or the palpable tension got to her. She paused, her eyes darting from Keir's rigid back to Rowena's face, obviously gauging the weather in the room and finding it dangerously volatile. She winced apologetically and started to retreat.

"It's all right, Fay. Bring it in," Keir commanded quietly. He turned to wave encouragement. "This is my secretary, Fay Pendleton. Mrs. Goodman, Fay."

"Pleased to meet you, Mrs. Goodman." The quick greeting was accompanied by a tentative smile.

"Yes. Thank you," Rowena returned jerkily, surprised by Keir's choice of secretary. Far from being a slickly sophisticated front person for him, this woman looked more like a homely pudding. Except for her hair. The rich burgundy colour with wide blonde bands had a definite touch of eccentricity.

The traymobile was swiftly wheeled to the table, and cups, saucers and plates were set out with deft efficiency. Black coffee was poured, milk and sugar placed handily, and a plate of artistically arranged sandwiches completed the service.

"Smoked salmon, turkey and avocado, ham and—"

"Thank you, Fay." Keir cut her off.

She gave Rowena a motherly look, her lively brown eyes kind. "Do try to eat."

"Fay..." Keir warned.

Rowena watched her leave, instinctively liking the woman and oddly comforted by the fact that she didn't emanate competitive sexiness. Not that it should matter what kind of woman Keir had close to him at work. It didn't, Rowena told herself. The contrast to Adriana Leigh was simply a relief.

The click of the door shutting behind Fay Pendleton jolted Rowena into realising she should have left, too. This brief hiatus didn't change anything. Coffee and sandwiches did not fix anything. In fact, they lent an absurd cloak of normality to a highly charged situation, one she should get out of right now before it developed into something worse.

She steeled herself to look at Keir again, thank him for the use of his office and escape from being alone with him any longer. With slow deliberation, she shifted her gaze from the door and met his squarely, determined to put an end to whatever he had in mind.

No matter what Phil had done, she was still married to him, and Keir had no right to be stirring feelings that should have been buried long ago. Buried along with her brother, Brett, because that had been the end of what they had shared together.

Whether he read her intention or not, Keir instantly forestalled any speech from her. "To answer your earlier question," he said in a tone of relentless pursuit, "I had no interest in Adriana because I don't care for manipulative people. I don't want to be with a woman whose responses aren't genuinely felt. It's a complete turn-off, regardless of how physically attractive and available she is.''

"And I'm suddenly a turn-on?"

The tense words hung between them, loaded with too much to back away from. Rowena was appalled at having been goaded into such a provocative retort. Somehow Keir's supreme confidence in who and what he was diminished Phil as a man, and she resented it. She resented even more the idea that Keir might think he could just step in and take advantage of her vulnerable state, letting her know he found her desirable even if her husband no longer did.

"No. Not suddenly," he answered quietly. "I doubt that many people forget their first love."

The yearning for that simpler time was in his eyes, and it hurt. It hurt because if he hadn't forgotten, he should have done something positive about it when it had really mattered. It hurt because it reminded her how naive and trusting she had been, the faith she'd had that he would come back to her and they'd make a life together.

It was he who had broken that faith, he who had dismissed his first love and put it behind him, and he had no right to call on it now. It was Phil who had brought love into her life again. Yet Phil was betraying that love, just as Keir had.

"It doesn't mean anything," she said desolately.

"It does to me."

She couldn't believe him, not after all this time. He might still be able to stir treacherous feelings in her, but his feelings could only be shallow, a response to present stimulus, nothing deep and lasting.

"How many years have we led separate lives, Keir?"

"We're still the same people, Rowena."

The burning conviction in his eyes riled her. "No, we're not. I'm not," she stated very deliberately, her conviction rising out of the pain of too many losses. *I'm scarred,* she wanted to yell at him, but pride held her tongue.

There was a shift in his expression. A frown. A doubt. "Do you really want Phil back, Rowena? Knowing what you now know about him and Adriana?"

It stung raw wounds. "He's my husband. He married me." *When you didn't.* "He's the father of my children," she added, then wished she had cut out her tongue before uttering those last words.

His face tightened. The sudden bleakness in his eyes smote her heart, awakening a painful guilt over the secret she had kept from him. His child . . . his son. But Keir had forfeited any right to Jamie. Phil was the only father Jamie had known, and Phil had been there for him, good to him. Only now . . . What should she do now? What if Adriana got her way and Phil didn't want to be bothered with Jamie any more?

Keir's gaze dropped to the table. He stepped over to it and lifted the milk jug. "Do you still have white with one sugar?'' he asked without looking up.

"I don't want coffee," she said flatly, wishing he hadn't remembered how she liked it. The familiarity hurt. Everything hurt. She should go. Why did she feel this heavy reluctance to move? What could be gained by continuing such a disturbing dialogue with Keir?

He slowly returned the jug to the table, then lifted his gaze directly to hers, his eyes having gathered a piercing intensity. "Do you want me to try to take Adriana away from Phil?"

That he should even think of making such a move for her stunned Rowena. "You said you didn't like manipulative people."

"I don't. Sometimes fire can only be fought with fire." He shrugged. "If it means so much to you to get Phil back..."

"No. Not that way." She inwardly recoiled at the awful dishonesty of it.

"If you really believe your happiness lies with him..."

"It wouldn't work anyway. Adriana's not stupid, Keir. You shouldn't have taken my hand."

Hand...body... She flushed again at the response his embrace had drawn from her. It wasn't fair that he could still affect her so deeply, so shatteringly.

"I'm sorry. I didn't mean to upset you," he said softly. Then with dry self-mockery, he continued, "I should have curbed my natural impulses."

"Maybe you meant no harm, but people put their own interpretations on things and reputations can be tainted. I don't want more trouble than I've got, Keir." She nodded to the door. "Your secretary could have come in while you were holding me. How would that have looked?"

She saw his eyes harden with weighing calculation. "You want Phil back," he said, as though planning how to achieve that end.

"I don't know what to do," she said miserably. She honestly didn't know how their marriage would work with the undermining spectre of adultery hovering between them, yet for the children's sake ...

"It could do some good to jolt him out of taking you for granted."

"How?" she asked without hope. Adriana had left her with no hope.

"I'm his boss. Most people would consider me a highly eligible bachelor. Adriana certainly saw me in that light," he said sardonically.

"What has this to do with me?" She didn't follow his train of thought at all.

"Sometimes people don't appreciate the value of what they have until someone takes it over, especially someone in a higher position than themselves. If we make a point of being seen together, you could use me to make him jealous, Rowena," Keir suggested without batting an eyelid. "You might find that Phil will suddenly want you again."

"If you think I'd start an affair with you..."
She was shocked speechless. It simply wasn't in
her to play tit for tat in the adultery game. And
Keir thought he knew her?

"I don't expect you to jump into bed with me.
We could obviously spend some time together.
We used to be friends, Rowena," he pressed,
giving her an appealing smile.

She stared at the smile. No, she thought, they
couldn't be friends. They had moved beyond
friendship. There was no doubt now that he remembered making love to her. And his attraction was far too potent. She'd be aware of him
all the time. It would muddle her up. Hopelessly.
And for what gain?

"I don't want to make Phil jealous. If he loses
faith in my commitment... Don't you see? It all
becomes too destructive. We'd have nothing
left."

The smile died, swallowed up by a dark,
blazing anger. "He doesn't deserve you."

"And you do?" The bubbling quagmire of
emotions inside her erupted. "What about the
women who've been in your life, Keir? The intimate relationships from which you've moved
on. And on. Why didn't any of them stick? Did
they mean as little as Adriana would if you
seduced her away from Phil?"

"No." Hot colour raced across his cheek-
bones. He made a slashing gesture with his hand.
"I wouldn't have touched Adriana. I was only
trying to see what you wanted, Rowena."

"What about the others?" she pressed, wanting to know, needing to know how he treated the women he had made love to. "I won't believe you've been celibate all these years."

"Of course I've sought what I needed. No one wants to be alone," he justified with passion. "I tried. I tried," he repeated, then shook his head in anguished hopelessness. "There was always something missing."

"So you dismissed them from your life."

"No. They're still friends."

You dismissed me. "Well, I won't be your friend, Keir. I'll never be your friend," she decided, her hurt deepened by the thought she had been the least of his women, someone he hadn't bothered to contact after the trauma of the accident had come between them.

"Rowena, please." He stepped towards her, hands reaching out.

"Don't come any closer, Keir," she fiercely warned. "Don't touch me. Ever again."

"I want to help. I want to—"

"No! I suppose it's some kind of compliment that I'm still desirable to you, but that's all it ever was. Only sex. You don't know the meaning of the word love. Or commitment."

"That's not true." His eyes burned into hers as though he was focusing his whole life force on her heart and mind. "Is it my fault that the woman I loved married someone else? That the children I wanted with her are Phil Goodman's?"

Her heart stopped. Her mind reeled. The world tilted, then slowly straightened. Her path was deadly clear. In a voice that shook with the strength of irrefutable knowledge, with all the pain she had once suffered for him, she delivered her judgment on Keir Delahunty, her eyes green daggers, stabbing home the fatal truth.

"I waited years for you. Years of faith and hope that gradually crumbled into the inevitable reality that what we'd shared was not important to you. Years, Keir. Years before I married Phil Goodman. Who gave me what you didn't give."

That stopped him. There was no comeback to those blunt facts. With a sense of having put the record absolutely straight and with adrenaline running high, Rowena moved forward, scooped her handbag from the chair where it had rested since before Adriana had arrived, skirted the shell-shocked figure of her first love and headed for the door into the corridor that bypassed the secretary's office.

"Rowena, stop! For God's sake! This doesn't make sense."

She whirled as she reached the door. "Liar! Liar!" she hurled at him.

It silenced him.

She opened the door and left him behind.

If she had to leave Phil behind her, she would do that, too. She didn't need a man in her life whom she couldn't trust.

But what about the children?

CHAPTER FIVE

"WHEN is Daddy coming home, Mummy?"

The unanswerable question. "I don't know, Emily," Rowena murmured as she bent to kiss her five-year-old daughter good night. Phil had not called her since he had left late last night, reinforcing his announcement that their marriage was over by walking out on her and going to Adriana Leigh.

"If it's soon, could I get up again? I want to show him my painting."

Emily was very much Daddy's girl, being Phil's first-born and favouring him in looks. Her fair hair was long, as her father liked it, and her blue eyes looked hopefully at Rowena, making her heart ache with the uncertainties that lay ahead of them.

"Darling, your painting is pinned to the corkboard," Rowena reminded her. "Daddy will see it when he comes home. Go to sleep now."

She dropped a soft kiss on her forehead. Emily sighed, disappointed, and Rowena wondered how scarred her young life would be without the father she adored on hand to provide her with the ever-ready support children needed.

Then Emily's little arms wound around Rowena's neck and she planted a big wet kiss on her cheek and said, "I love you, Mummy," and Rowena's heart turned over. Perhaps having a mother was enough if the bond was kept strong. In today's world there were many single parents coping successfully with the problems she would face if Phil didn't come back.

"I love you too, Emily," she whispered. "Good night."

Emily snuggled into her pillow, and Rowena tucked the bedclothes around her, fighting back the tears that pricked her eyes. She quickly crossed the room to check Sarah, who had dropped asleep during their bedtime story. It was fortunate that today had been one of her two days a week at a local playgroup. Sarah was quite a precocious three-year-old, and Rowena had been grateful to have her bright little girl occupied with other children while she grappled with grim realities.

A strand of long brown hair was still curled around the finger that habitually twiddled with it. Her thumb rested slackly in her mouth. Still a baby, despite her surprising astuteness. Very gently, Rowena removed the thumb and untwined the hair. Sarah didn't so much as twitch, tired out from playing games all day. Would she miss her father as much as Emily would?

It was easy for Adriana Leigh to say the girls were young enough to get over the separation without any lasting trauma. She was far enough removed to neither know nor care. What worried

Rowena was how much Adriana was influencing Phil's thinking about it.

Yet how could Phil not miss his family? He hadn't been the kind of man who ignored his children. If anything, he had been on the indulgent side, leaving any disciplinary measures to her.

Best Daddy in the world.

Had that stroked his ego?

She shook off Keir's insidious criticism of Phil's character and walked quickly to the door. She cast one last maternal look over her daughters settled peacefully in their twin beds. They didn't have to be told anything yet. Phil might change his mind.

Two more days and school was finished for the year. Then Christmas only a week later. There wasn't much time for Phil to have second thoughts. How could she possibly explain his absence to three children who expected their father to be with them for Christmas?

Having quietly closed the girls' bedroom door, Rowena took a deep breath, hoping to lower her anxiety level before facing Jamie again. Being ten, he stayed up later than the girls, and he'd been unnaturally quiet over dinner, watching her as though he sensed something wrong. She hadn't given him much attention. He reminded her too painfully of Keir tonight. And the memories that had been evoked earlier today.

She had to shut that out of her mind, concentrate on other things. No good could come from thinking about Keir and what he'd said and how he had reacted to her. She could not delude herself with might-have-beens. If he hadn't lied to her... But he had, and she couldn't forgive him that patently false declaration. She had to be strong now, strong enough to stand alone if need be.

She had left Jamie watching television in the family room. As she headed for the kitchen she realised the house was quiet, no noise at all. Perhaps Jamie had his head in a book. He loved reading. Rowena hoped that was the case. It would leave her free to ponder what course she should take next.

He was sitting on a bar stool at the counter that divided the kitchen from the family room. A book was open in front of him, a glass of milk half-drunk at hand. He looked up as Rowena entered the room, and she had an instant flash of Keir, assessing her with weighing calculation. The expression was shockingly the same.

"Good book?" she forced herself to ask lightly, crossing to the sink to fill the electric jug for coffee.

No reply.

She flicked him an inquiring look as she reached for the jug. "What's going on, Mum?" Serious, direct and determined.

Rowena's heart fluttered. She swiftly switched her attention to the tap, turning it on, running water. "Well, the girls are settled for the night."

"I mean about Dad."

Rowena's heart squeezed tight. How could Jamie guess that something was wrong? She thought she'd covered up reasonably well so far. "What do you want to know, Jamie?" she asked, evading his keen gaze by putting the jug on to boil and spooning coffee into a mug.

"I heard you crying last night. It sounded awful. I didn't know what to do. I thought Dad was with you and I shouldn't butt in. But when I got up this morning he wasn't here. And he hasn't come home tonight, either."

The blunt statement of facts was recited in a tightly controlled voice that tried so hard to be calm and sensible it moved Rowena to tears again. Jamie was only ten, yet here he was, manfully taking the bull by the horns in his concern for her. He must have been worrying all day, poor darling, and she hadn't wanted to see it.

Well, there was no hiding the truth now. Jamie wouldn't be fobbed off with soothing platitudes. Yet to tell the whole truth might damn Phil in his eyes for a long time. A surge of white-hot anger helped restore her composure. Did Phil even begin to comprehend what damage he was doing, getting his ego stroked by that woman?

"Mum?"

Jamie had to be answered. What was the best line to tread? She put down the coffee spoon and turned to face him, seeing for the first time the underlying anxiety in his eyes. It made her want to weep again. Why were the innocent made victims of other people's desires and pain?

"I'm sorry for upsetting you with my crying, Jamie. Your father and I had an argument. Parents sometimes do, you know."

He nodded gravely, but he wasn't satisfied. "I've never heard you cry like that. It went on for a long time."

She thought of him lying in the dark, listening, and was ashamed of letting herself go so much. It had felt as though her whole world was breaking up, ending, but it wasn't really. It was going to be a different world whether Phil came back or not. It could never be the same again. She recognised that now. But she would cope with it. Somehow.

"Things change, Jamie," she said sadly. "Sometimes it's not easy to accept the change."

His face suddenly assumed a bullish expression, and his eyes took on a fierce glitter. "Has Dad gone off to another woman?"

She was shocked. "What makes you think that?" The words tripped off her tongue, not in denial, simply in appalled wonder that he had leapt to so much. Or had he heard part of their argument?

"Half the kids in my class have divorced parents. I get to hear things." He looked too wise. "Dad's been coming home late and not here most of the weekends."

"Work. He's had a lot of work to do." That was the excuse Phil had given.

"Why isn't he home tonight?"

"Because he ... wants to be somewhere else," she finished limply.

"Is he coming back?" Hard suspicion, giving no quarter.

"I don't know." She couldn't lie to him. On the other hand, the trouble with saying anything more was that it couldn't be unsaid later, and Rowena didn't want Jamie completely alienated from Phil. "If you don't mind, Jamie, I'd rather not talk about this right now. Your father and I ... We need some time to work things out. Okay?"

He considered for several moments before nodding. "Okay, Mum." Then with a flash of fierce feeling, "I just want you to know that whatever Dad does, you'll always have me."

"Oh, Jamie ..."

She heard her voice waver and swallowed hard. Before she could speak again, Jamie was off the stool, around the counter and flinging his arms around her waist, his head pressing against her breasts as he hugged her hard. So loyal, so protective, so intensely loving. Her hands curled around his head, fingers stroking his hair. Her son, Keir's son. If only Keir had been worthy of him.

"I don't want you to cry like that any more, Mum," came the muffled plea, revealing his deep inner distress at her breakdown.

"I won't, Jamie," she gently promised him. "I was feeling very alone. But I'm not really alone, am I?"

"No. You've got me."

"And I'll never forget that again. Thank you for reminding me."

"That's okay."

What courage he had! Courage, resolution, caring. Rowena savoured the comforting warmth of holding him, her boy holding her. For the past year or so he had shied away from "soppy stuff." He didn't seem to mind it right now, but she didn't want him to start feeling awkward about it.

"What are you reading?" she asked.

His head came up and his arms dropped. "It's a book about rabbits called *Watership Down*."

She slid her hands to his shoulders and smiled. "Why don't you take it to bed and read it there? I'm going to watch TV for a while."

"Will you be all right by yourself, Mum?"

"I'll be fine," she assured him warmly. "Light out at nine o'clock, remember."

He collected his book, said good night and went off with the jaunty confidence of having settled what needed to be settled.

Rowena wished that life could be so simple. She made herself a mug of coffee, switched on the television, sank into her usual armchair and idly flicked through the channels, stopping at what appeared to be a documentary on train travel. What was on the screen was irrelevant, its only purpose to provide a semblance of normality to the evening in case Jamie checked on her.

Her mind ran endlessly over memories of her marriage, both good and bad, sifting through what had contributed to the highs and the lows. She found her thoughts coloured by the opinions given by Adriana and Keir, especially Keir's, despite her efforts not to think of him.

You want a husband who needs to be rescued from another woman?

She didn't. She wanted a husband who would always put her first. As Adriana had pointed out, she was guilty of putting the children first at times, but they were Phil's children as well as hers. They certainly weren't another man.

The problem was, even if Phil did come back to her, Rowena didn't think she could ever feel right with him again. And that could only lead to more problems. Whichever way she looked at it, there were unhappy times ahead.

A noise caught her attention. Was that the front door opening...and closing?

CHAPTER SIX

Rowena hurriedly clicked off the television set and pushed herself to her feet. Phil—it had to be—come home. Yes, footsteps heading for the kitchen. What did it mean?

She glanced at her watch. Nine-forty. He'd waited until the children were asleep. Out of the way. Maybe he found it easier to face her without a watching audience, especially if he intended to admit a mistake.

She moved unsteadily towards the counter where Jamie had sat, instinctively wanting something solid separating her and the man who had betrayed his commitment to her and their family. She felt defensive, although she told herself she had no reason to be. It was he who had put their marriage under threat.

She also shied away from the thought of being touched. Phil had undoubtedly come from Adriana. If he reached out for her now... No, she couldn't bear it, not with the image of Adriana so fresh in her mind.

Phil came into the kitchen in aggressive mode. It wasn't hard to see he was not bent on reconciliation. He glared at her, his blue eyes ablaze with fury. "What the hell do you think you were

doing, going to Delahunty's today?'' he demanded in a voice laced with outrage.

It was like a punch in the stomach. Didn't he
realise how desperate she'd been to put herself
on the line against his other woman? Didn't it
tell him how much their marriage meant to her?
Was there no appreciation at all of what she was
going through because of him?

''I wanted to see the woman you prefer to me
and the children,'' she answered, needing to focus
his mind on the real issue.

It floated over his head. ''To go to my boss...
God damn it, Rowena! You put me in an invi-
dious position, dragging Keir into this.''

The realisation hit her that this rage was about
appearances. She had made him look bad in his
boss's eyes. That was what had brought him here.
Not her and the children. Phil hated looking bad.

A great distance yawned between them as she
totted up the clean-cut handsome face, the perfectly groomed dark blonde hair, the buttoned-
down collar of his expensive white shirt, the silk
tie perfectly in place, the smartly tailored double-
breasted suit that was an up-to-date fashion
statement. It had always been so very important
to Phil to look good. She had been proud of him
looking good. She hadn't known it was more important to him than her and the children.

''Emily wanted to show you her latest
painting,'' she said, waving to the corkboard on
the wall above the kitchen counter, hoping it
would jolt him out of his self-centredness.

He didn't spare it so much as a glance. "Don't drag the children into this. I want to know what went on between you and Keir Delahunty."

Jealous? Was Keir right about jealousy bringing Phil to heel? She frowned. It was so grubby, somehow.

"You were with him before and after you saw Adriana," he went on in fuming accusation.

Rowena instinctively minimised what had happened. "We met accidentally in the car park. He knew about you and Adriana. He guessed why I'd come. He offered his office for privacy."

"Why should he do that?"

"To prevent an unpleasant scene. More gossip."

"Adriana said he was holding your hand. And he took your side. I'm one of his top executives, and he's hardly met you. Why should he care about you? Tell me that!"

Had Keir really cared, or was he an opportunist like Adriana? Rowena felt wretchedly confused about Keir's motives. Perhaps he regretted not having pursued her. And the attraction was still there. If he hadn't lied... That was the killing point.

"He knows me from a long time ago," she said quietly, trying to defuse Phil's anger and suspicion. "Our families were once friends."

A fierce resentment flared. "You never mentioned this before. I've been working with him for almost two years, and neither you nor he has ever referred to having known each other."

She shrugged. "I imagine he didn't want to re-member it any more than I did. The friendship ended when my brother died in Keir's car. My parents blamed Keir."

"Was he guilty?"

Rowena hated the speculative spark in Phil's eyes. Did he want to hold something over Keir? "No, he wasn't. It was an accident. Brett was driving. My parents were too distraught to accept that it was Brett's fault. As they saw it, if Keir's parents hadn't given him a sports car and if he hadn't let Brett drive it, the accident wouldn't have happened."

"Then he should feel bitter towards you, not— Hold on a moment." He was clearly struck by another train of thought. "Weren't you sev-enteen when your brother died?"

"Yes. As I said, a long time ago."

"When was it exactly?"

"New Year's Day." The memory was still stark, the shock, the grief— Brett and Keir, and the guilty relief that Keir was still alive. Still alive now, and making more trouble for her. She shouldn't have gone to his office, shouldn't have stayed talking to him.

Phil's fist crashed down on the counter. "He's the father, isn't he?"

The yelled words rang in her ears. She looked at Phil's furiously pugnacious face and was too stunned to make any reply.

"Jamie's birthday is in September, nine months after the accident that killed your brother. Oh, it adds up now, doesn't it?'' Phil jeered. ''That's why Jamie's father didn't stand by you. Your parents blamed Keir Delahunty for your brother's death and sent you off to your aunt in Queensland.''

He flung up his hands and swung away from her, marching around the kitchen, smacking his fist into his other hand. ''And you let me take a job with the father of your son,'' he shouted at her in savage condemnation.

Rowena snapped herself out of the shock of Phil tying Keir to her pregnancy. ''Jamie is your son. *Your* son,'' she cried in a desperate attempt to set things straight. ''You're the only father he's known. Please stop this. It has nothing to do with—''

''Nothing?'' he shouted. ''You call it nothing for you to fob Keir Delahunty's son onto me?''

''Jamie is my son. And you adopted him as yours,'' she countered fiercely.

''Well, he's not any more.''

She couldn't believe this. How could he turn on Jamie as though their father-and-son relationship had meant nothing? ''That's very convenient, Phil. Are you going to suggest the girls have other fathers, too?'' she demanded heatedly.

''Leave them out of this.''

''You keep saying that, but you can't leave them out. Or is that what you really want? Not to think about them. Grasping any excuse not to think about Jamie.''

"All these years, keeping it a secret from me..."

"All these years you haven't been the least bit concerned about who Jamie's biological father is. You looked after him, cared about him, played with him. You were proud to own him as your son. How do you wipe it all out, Phil? Tell me that!"

He flushed, evading her gaze for a moment, then swinging back to turn guilt into anger again. "You had no right not to tell me before I accepted the job at Delahunty's."

"You wanted the job. It was a feather in your cap. I wanted you to be happy. If I'd known it would lead to your meeting Adriana Leigh and deserting all of us for her—"

"I have every intention of remaining a father to Emily and Sarah."

At least he had that much conscience, Rowena thought, wondering where the rest of it was. "So it's only Jamie you're going to dump," she said, wanting to bludgeon every shred of his conscience into reviewing what he was doing. "Is it because Adriana doesn't want to be bothered with him? Little girls are much more malleable for a woman like her. Or maybe you haven't got the guts for answering sticky questions from Jamie."

The flush deepened. "I haven't heard you deny he's Keir Delahunty's bastard kid."

Rowena seethed over that demeaning phrase. She barely held herself back from flying at him tooth and claw. "I don't have to deny anything," she fired at him. "You adopted Jamie in good faith. You just want to muddy things up so you'll feel justified in what you're doing, and you have no justification. None at all!"

He slapped his hands on the counter and leaned towards her in belligerent challenge. "Look me straight in the eye, Rowena, and deny that you and Keir Delahunty were lovers and that Jamie is his natural son."

She stared at him, hating the feeling of being cornered, hating all the connotations he was putting on a love affair that ended long before she had met Phil and married him, and hating his evasion of responsibilities he had willingly taken on.

Even so, she couldn't bring herself to lie. In some strange way she felt a pride in Jamie's natural heritage and didn't want to deny it. After all, Keir Delahunty had certainly made his way in the world. He was also Phil's boss, hardly a comedown in the genetic pool. Yet to make a claim...

"Keir doesn't know. He doesn't know," she repeated with passionate emphasis.

"Well, maybe he ought to know." Phil straightened up, a triumphant gleam in his eyes. "Maybe he should take over the support of the boy I've been supporting all these years."

"No," she gasped, appalled that he should even think it.

He looked smug, in control. "Stay out of my business, Rowena. That's my territory. And Adriana's. And I don't want you messing with it."

"So it's all right to keep working for Keir now, is it?" she snapped bitterly.

"He doesn't know, and you don't want him told. That puts me in the driver's seat."

He was feeling good again. It was crazy. He was disowning a son who had done nothing to deserve rejection, and believing he held some kind of trump card over her and Keir. What kind of twisted thinking was that? Rowena couldn't relate to it.

He shook a finger at her. "No more putting Adriana on the spot. Keep out of our lives, Rowena. I told you last night you can keep this house. You've got a home for yourself and the children. That's more than fair."

She supposed she had to concede it was generous, though there was no telling how long the spirit of generosity would last once Adriana got to work on him.

"I'll be seeing a solicitor tomorrow," he informed her. "I don't want any hassle about reasonable access to my daughters."

Her heart bled for Jamie, but what could she do against such unfair intransigence? What more could she say? "That's it, is it, Phil? All that we had together has come to an end?"

Guilt flickered briefly in his eyes. "You were the wrong woman for me, Rowena. I'm sorry, but that's the truth."

"How was I wrong? You didn't think I was wrong when you married me. When did I change?"

"You didn't change."

"Then explain it to me, Phil. I need to know where I failed."

He heaved a discomforted sigh. "You were what I thought I wanted in a wife. It just didn't turn out how I visualised it."

"I don't understand," she pleaded.

He grimaced but went on reluctantly. "Well, you represented the ideal I had in my mind. You were happy for me to be the breadwinner, happy to have children and make a home for us, looking after everything on the domestic side."

"You saw me as the old-fashioned housewife."

"With the family. The whole bit. I hadn't had it. You know my parents were divorced," he said tersely.

And he was about to visit that upon his own children, Rowena thought grimly.

"And you're quite beautiful in your own way," he grudgingly conceded. "I was proud to have you at my side."

"Then why? Why let it all go?" she cried in anguished bewilderment.

"I told you. It was good for a while, but it's not what I want now."

"You believe Adriana is better for you?"

"It's not just Adriana," he said petulantly. "I want freedom. I want stimulation, excitement, the fun of doing things with spontaneity instead of having to live up to your ideals."

"By fun I assume you mean infidelity."

Anger bloomed again. "You expected too much of me. I'm tired of it. I want out. Is that clear enough for you?"

"Yes. Thank you."

It all made sense now. She had been Phil's fantasy. His mistake was in underestimating how much he needed to put into his role for the fantasy to become real. Looking good wasn't enough.

"So you're just walking out and leaving me to it," she said flatly, having had any last bit of caring for Phil drained out of her.

He shrugged. "You've gained a home, remember. And you'll find someone else. You're still young and attractive." He turned his back on her and walked towards the door as though she'd never been anything to him.

It struck a vengeful streak in Rowena. "Maybe I'll find Keir Delahunty. How will you like that?"

He stopped, his back rigid. Rowena knew he didn't like it one bit. He swung a glittering gaze to her. "Try it, Rowena, and this house won't be yours. It will be sold, and I'm entitled to half the proceeds."

She bit down on her wayward tongue. She had to consider the children's welfare. Wild threats were only self-defeating. She had no intention of inviting Keir Delahunty back into her life.

Satisfied he had won his point, Phil walked out. Rowena didn't follow him to the front door. She wouldn't follow him anywhere anymore. He had severed the last sense of bonding with him.

CHAPTER SEVEN

KEIR DELAHUNTY gave up trying to concentrate on work. There was too much on his mind, and telling himself that none of it was his business didn't help one iota. He rolled his chair away from the drawing board, stood up and strolled around his office, ending up where Rowena had been yesterday, behind the table, looking down at the streets of Chatswood.

He'd had to tell Phil about her visit. It would have been unnatural not to when he'd come to give his report on the Pyrmont warehouse. Adriana would have had no qualms about telling him. Phil's embarrassment, the barely suppressed anger in his eyes did not bode well for Rowena.

Had she suffered a backlash from him last night?

Keir groaned inwardly. The frustration of not being able to help, not being able to go to her was eating into him. Phil didn't want her. Rowena had no reason to still feel committed to him and their marriage. How could she keep loving him in the face of such demeaning infidelity? Surely it was impossible.

His mind replayed every minute he'd spent with her yesterday, the words spoken, the tension, the eye contact. When he'd held her, he'd had such a strong sense of connecting with her again, but her rejection had been so swift, so vehement, maybe he'd been fooling himself.

Nevertheless, he didn't believe her conflict with Phil was entirely responsible for her intensely emotional responses to him. She might not want to acknowledge it, but the attraction was still there, surging between them.

Liar...

He shook his head. The word kept ringing in his ears, a death knell to any hope of recapturing what he'd once had with Rowena. But it wasn't true. If there had been a lie, it wasn't his.

He could still remember the sickening emptiness he'd felt when Rowena's mother had shown him the photograph, a totally devastating reinforcement of her father's insistence that their daughter didn't want him in her life and to stay right out of it and not bring her any more grief.

He'd stared disbelievingly at the photograph, Rowena with a baby on her lap, a man crouched adoringly beside them. Married, her parents had said, married to a good man, mother of a fine baby boy and happily settled in Queensland. There was no place for Keir Delahunty in any of their lives.

It had to have been a lie if Rowena had waited years for him. And he couldn't disbelieve her. He couldn't forget the blazing passion in her eyes as she had accused him, condemned him for having done what Phil Goodman was doing to her now, betraying her love, deserting her.

It must have been someone else's baby she'd been holding, simply a fortuitous photograph her parents had maliciously used to get rid of him. Or to give him the pain of loss they felt. As though losing his best friend and suffering through all those operations to walk again wasn't enough, Keir thought bitterly. They'd made him lose Rowena, too.

Vengeance, indeed. And for what? Brett had almost killed him, as well as himself. If that dog hadn't run onto the road... Keir shut his eyes tight, wanting to erase the memory of the last frantic moments before the car had crashed. Better to forget everything. But he couldn't.

Liar...

Would Rowena believe him about the photograph? Did she believe he'd written to her? He had no evidence to back up either claim. At least she didn't blame him for Brett's death. That was one small comfort, although it didn't balance the rest of the ledger against him. Was his word enough to get past her distrust?

The telephone on his desk rang.

He swung around in irritation. He'd told Fay to take all his calls this morning. Why wasn't she handling this? He was tempted not to answer, but there had to be a cogent reason for her to disobey his instructions, and he trusted Fay's judgment. He strode to his workstation and snatched up the receiver.

"What is it?"

"You have a visitor."

"I said no appointments."

"Keir, you remember yesterday when I brought in the coffee and sandwiches?"

"What are you getting at Fay?"

"I'm very sensitive to vibrations, you know. I think you'll want to see this visitor."

"Who is it?"

"Mrs. Goodman's son. He's come to see you. Very specifically you, Keir. He does not intend to go away until he does see you."

That knocked the wind out of any further protest and triggered a buzz of questions. Why would Rowena's son come here? To him? Where was Phil? What was happening to Rowena?

"Bring him in, Fay." The quiet command belied the turmoil in his mind.

He put down the receiver, hesitated over where best to place himself to meet the boy, then moved out of the workstation to greet him as he entered.

Fay opened the connecting door to her office and waved forward a schoolboy—eight, nine, ten? Surely too tall to be any younger. Black hair like Rowena's. He didn't have her green eyes. They were similar in shape but they were hazel. He was smartly dressed in a school uniform and carrying what was obviously his school bag.

He should be in his classroom right now, Keir thought. His parents undoubtedly believed he was. Yet there was no trace of guilt or concern in the boy's expression about having his truancy found out. He looked directly at Keir, curiously, assessingly, as though measuring him against some preconceived image.

"Jamie, this is Mr. Delahunty. Jamie Goodman, Keir." Fay introduced them, giving Keir a roll of her eyes that clearly said, Well, the fat's in the fire now, and this is what you get for involving yourself in other people's intimate problems.

Keir stepped forward, smiled encouragingly and offered his hand. "How do you do, Jamie?" Rowena's son. Another chance to reach her?

The boy put down his bag and gravely took his hand. "I'm pleased to meet you, sir."

Drilled in good manners. He didn't show any pleasure in the meeting. No responding smile. He seemed caught up in studying Keir's face, feature by feature.

"Please see that we aren't interrupted, Fay," Keir instructed and gave her a nod of approval for making an exception to orders for Rowena's son. "Thank you."

She left them together.

Jamie withdrew his hand and his scrutiny and cast his questing gaze around Keir's office. "Is this all yours?" he asked.

"All mine," Keir affirmed. "I designed it, as well. Would you like a tour?"

A flash of keen interest. "Yes, please."

Keir wondered how many tests he had to pass before Jamie Goodman revealed why he was here.

He proceeded to explain the purpose of all his architect's tools in his workstation, demonstrated how the drawing board could be adjusted, showed how he drew visualisations of his designs on the computer and answered a comprehensive range of intelligent questions. The boy was extremely bright.

"How old are you, Jamie?" Keir asked as he ushered him over to the model display.

It earned another speculative look. "How old are you?"

Keir had to smile at such a direct retort. "I'm thirty-five."

Jamie frowned, "That makes you older than—" He clamped down on whatever comparison he had been about to make and turned to examine the models.

Apparently the subject of age was not to be pursued, yet Keir was tantalised by it. Rowena had stated she had waited years for him. If that were the case, this boy could only be eight at most, yet he looked and sounded older.

"I've seen this one. It's been built at Manly," Jamie remarked, pleased at recognising the town houses Rowena had commented on yesterday.

"Yes. Your mother said she liked the design."

Jamie moved on to the next model. "Do you like my mum?"

The question sounded offhand but Keir knew intuitively it wasn't. "Yes, I do. We were close friends once. Unfortunately, your mother's brother was killed in a car accident. I was injured in the same crash. My parents flew me to the United States for special medical treatment, and I didn't see your mother again for a long time.''

The boy was still, not looking at Keir, but the sense of him weighing every word Keir said was very strong. ''What did you need treatment for?'' he asked.

''My pelvis and both my legs were broken in many places. There was some doubt I would ever walk again.''

Jamie turned and looked at Keir's legs. ''How long did it take for you to mend?''

''Eighteen months.''

Jamie nodded as though the answer met whatever check list he had in his mind. ''You must have been badly smashed up,'' he remarked sympathetically.

Keir grimaced. ''It wasn't much fun.''

''No, I guess it wasn't.'' Jamie's eyes travelled up in open assessment of Keir's physical condition. ''You're okay now, though,'' he decided.

''In top shape,'' Keir agreed.

Jamie pointed to the glass wall across the room. ''Do you mind if I have a look at the view?''

''You're welcome.''

Keir watched him walk around the table and stand where his mother had stood, looking out. It was uncanny. He wondered how close the bond was between mother and son.

''You sure can see a lot,'' the boy said appreciatively.

"It also gives me plenty of natural light," Keir answered, playing along with the game of not hastening to the purpose of the visit.

"Are you and Mum friends now?"

The question caught Keir unprepared, and it was loaded with pitfalls. What was behind it? Had there been an argument between Phil and Rowena last night, heated words that Jamie had overheard and possibly misconstrued? Keir swiftly decided that honesty was the best policy.

"I would like to be friends, Jamie," he said slowly, "but I don't think your mother feels the same way."

"Why not?"

As an inquisitor, Jamie Goodman was excelling at putting Keir on the spot. "Well, there's your father," Keir started tentatively.

"He's not my father."

The hard, vehement denial stunned Keir into turbulent silence. His mind leapt into overdrive. Rowena had had an illegitimate child? When? By whom? The man in the photograph? His back had been turned to the camera, unidentifiable. But if he was the father, Rowena had not waited. Unless the pregnancy had resulted from ... from an act of rape.

Keir was inwardly recoiling from this last thought when Jamie swung around, an oddly adult look of set determination on his young face. Keir was reminded of not Rowena but...

"I'm ten years old."

"Ten," Keir repeated, still trying to pinpoint the familiarity.

"My birthday is the twenty-eighth of September," the boy stated with portentous emphasis.

The date sent Keir's mind reeling.

"And *you* are my father."

CHAPTER EIGHT

IT WAS best to keep busy, Rowena told herself, setting out all the ingredients for the Christmas pudding. Apart from which, just because Phil would not be with them for Christmas didn't mean that anything else had to change. She would proceed as though everything were normal. It would be less upsetting for the children if they saw her carrying on as usual.

"Sultanas for me, please, Mummy?"

She smiled at Sarah, wriggling excitely on the stool behind the kitchen counter, her big green eyes agog at all the fruit that went into a pudding. "In a minute, darling. Wait until I weigh what I need, and then you can have what's left in the packet. Okay?"

"Okay." Blissful contentment.

Sarah was so easily pleased, delighted with the world and everything in it. Rowena hoped her bright little girl's happy outlook on life wouldn't be too dimmed by her father's absence.

Emily would take it the worst. She would need a lot of loving reassurance. Her disappointment when Phil wasn't here again this morning had put her in a sulky mood. She had started to whine about Daddy being away too much. Jamie had cut her off, telling her to stop acting like a baby and get ready for school.

Jamie, the man of the house, protecting her.

Rowena sighed. She couldn't let Jamie shoulder her burdens. Emily had to be told the situation. They each had to be told. Was it better done all together or separately?

Rowena pondered the problem as she poured sultanas onto the kitchen scales. Having measured the right quantity, she tipped them into the mixing bowl and handed the largely emptied packet to Sarah. The currants were another simple measuring job, but the raisins, dates and cherries needed cutting up.

After considerable thought, Rowena decided to leave the dreaded announcement for one more day. The school term finished tomorrow. She didn't want Emily upset in front of her friends and classmates. This was strictly a family problem, and it was better for Emily to have the whole Christmas vacation to come to terms with it.

As for Jamie... Rowena sighed again. How was she going to tell him his father didn't want him any more?

The door chimes sounded.

"I'll go, Mummy," Sarah cried eagerly, scrambling off the stool in her hurry to greet a visitor.

But who was visiting? Rowena wasn't expecting anyone. "Wait, Sarah. We need to wash our hands first."

A quick trip to the sink, and the stickiness of the fruit was removed from both sets of hands. The door chimes rang again. Rowena hastily threw a cloth over the mixing bowl. She glanced at the wall clock as she ushered Sarah out of the kitchen. Almost lunchtime. Who would be calling at this hour? Well, there was only one way to find out.

Sarah skipped down the hallway ahead of her but pulled up in the foyer, waiting for Rowena. The front door was always kept locked for security. There were two shapes visible through the stained-glass panels. One was considerably shorter than the other, about the same height as Jamie, in fact. For some reason this was reassuring. With her sense of apprehension fading, Rowena opened the door.

Shock hit her like a cannon ball.

Keir Delahunty and Jamie together. Keir, eyeing her with steady resolution, holding Jamie's hand as his claim of passage. Jamie, who should be at school, looking at her with an air of triumphant satisfaction.

"He knows. I told him," her son announced as though it was a deed well done. "He's going to help you, Mum."

"May I come in, Rowena?" Keir's request was politely put, but he emanated an air of relentless purpose that clearly said no amount of wild horses would drag him away.

"Who's he?" Sarah inquired of her older brother.

"His name is Keir Delahunty and he's my real father," Jamie declared with pride.

Rowena closed her eyes. She felt the blood drain from her face as her world spun out of control. Keir's voice rang in her ears. "Jamie, look after your little sister. Your mother needs to sit down." An arm came around her waist, hugging her close to a wall of warmth and strength, supporting her as she was walked into the lounge and settled onto the closest armchair. "Head down, Rowena."

"What's wrong with Mum?" Jamie demanded in alarm.

"A little faint, I think. Nothing serious," Keir answered. "Did she eat any breakfast this morning?"

"I didn't see her have anything except coffee."

"Mummy's making a Christmas pudding," Sarah supplied helpfully.

"Jamie, could you make your mother a cup of coffee and find some biscuits or cake for her?"

"Sure I can. You'll look after Mum?"

"Yes."

"I want some biscuits, too, Jamie."

Rowena lifted her head, her eyes clearing enough to see Sarah trailing after her brother, leaving her alone with Keir.

"Take a few deep breaths, Rowena," he advised gently. "I'll just go and shut the front door so everything's secure."

Secure? Rowena felt a bubble of hysteria rising and hastily clamped down on it. Her mind whirled around the realisation that Jamie must have eavesdropped on all that had been said between her and Phil last night, and bringing Keir into their lives was his solution to the situation. But it was no solution at all. It was a massive complication!

Then Keir was back, crouching in front of her, taking her hands, rubbing them between his.

"I'm all right," she croaked.

"I'm sorry about the shock, Rowena. There was no easy way."

Concern and caring in his voice. Of course he cared! He'd just been presented with a son, hadn't he? Jamie would impress anyone as a boy a man would be proud of fathering. Any man except Phil! And now everything was going to be ten times worse.

"Jamie shouldn't have—"

"He had your interests at heart, Rowena."

She looked up wildly, her eyes filled with chaotic torment. "Then he's hopelessly mistaken, isn't he?"

Keir held her gaze steadily. "Give me the chance to show he's not."

"Phil threatened to sell this home and put us out of it if I got involved with you. Even if I wanted you, I can't afford you in our lives, Keir."

"I'll give you a home that no one else can sell. I'll put it in your name. Absolute security of tenure."

It was a mind-boggling offer, too big to be believed, tossed off as though it was the easiest thing in the world for him to do. She stared at him, the seeds of mistrust growing, multiplying. Was it another grandiose lie to impress her?

"Why on earth should you do that?" she asked suspiciously.

His gaze didn't waver, direct, intense, compelling. "If for no other reason, I owe it to you and Jamie."

Maybe he felt some indebtedness right now. Rowena could accept that he did. But things changed when it came down to the nitty-gritty. Phil had left her in no doubt of that.

"You're in the first flush of finding out you have a son, Keir. What about tomorrow and tomorrow and tomorrow? How long will the sense of responsibility last?"

"For the rest of my life," he said quietly.

She wanted to believe it. She wanted to but she couldn't. She wrenched her eyes from his and looked at her hands, still warmly enfolded. She pulled them out of his grasp and shrank into the deeply cushioned armchair, frightened of letting him get too close to her. It was too tempting to swallow the dream he was offering.

"I've heard promises before. I'm sitting in the middle of broken promises," she said, more to herself than him. "I think I'd rather manage my own life than count on support that doesn't stay true."

He stood up, very tall, very formidable, rock solid in his purpose. "There is Jamie to consider, Rowena."

"And my other children," she fiercely insisted, her maternal instinct rushing to the fore. "I won't have my children separated by fathers who only care about their own. If you think you can overlook the rest of my family in your plans for a future with Jamie—"

"I have no intention of overlooking anything. Not this time," he said grimly.

"What is that supposed to mean?"

"It means I want you in my life, Rowena. I want Jamie in my life. I don't want to lose out on any part of either of you. And that includes your daughters, Jamie's sisters."

She steeled herself against any melting towards him. "I heard the same from Phil. About Jamie. Only now it suits him to disown the son he adopted." The still raw pain of that rejection flashed out at Keir. "We're not pieces of baggage to be passed around."

"I'm not Phil."

He was right. Keir was more powerful, more self-assured, more focused on her and her needs than Phil had ever been. And probably more capable of answering them. She didn't doubt he had the wealth to buy her a house. She suspected he was harbouring the expectation of living in it with her, too. Yet he couldn't want her that much. It had to be the idea of having Jamie that was spurring him on to such sweeping declarations.

"You think you can just walk in here and take over me and my family?" she asked, trying to gauge how far he had considered what he was doing.

"No, I don't. I think I have to earn those privileges."

"It will take a lot of earning, Keir," she warned.

"I'm not acting on impulse, Rowena. I've had many years to consider what is meaningful in my life. I don't come here lightly."

He looked unshakable.

She remembered how convincing he had been about his love for her all those years ago. It hadn't proven true. Words were easy. They were also empty unless backed up by real substance.

On the other hand, maybe she was being too harsh, too sweeping in her demands. Expecting too much. Ideals were fine, but when they didn't work, compromises had to be made. Jamie was entitled to have a father in his life, and since Phil had abdicated the role, why not Keir? He could give Jamie more advantages in a material sense than she ever could alone. But if he let Jamie down, as he had let her down...

"Are you sure you want to be father to Jamie, Keir?"

"Yes."

"Are you aware of how much it costs to bring up a child, physically, financially and emotionally?"

"Whatever it takes, I'll meet it."

His confidence niggled her. He was untried, inexperienced, and words were cheap. Promises were cheap. "In that case you won't mind making provision for him," she said, driven to make him realise the consequences of commitment.

"No problem."

Put him to the test, a mutinous little voice whispered. "As an act of good faith, you could open a trust account for Jamie that will cover his keep and his education," Rowena rattled off. "When you show me how committed you are to being his father and all it entails, I'll agree to your seeing Jamie on a regular basis."

He didn't so much as blink. "And you, Rowena?"

"I come at a higher price," she said loftily, determined to test him to the limit. "You see, I've been supposedly loved and discarded once too often. You'll have to buy me a house of my own before I even begin to think of involving myself with you on any personal basis."

He observed the hard glitter in her eyes for several moments before answering her challenge. "Would you then begin to think, Rowena, or is this simply an act of vengeance for what you've suffered?"

Was it vengeance? She hesitated, not liking that image of herself. No, it was common sense, the little voice whispered. To let herself be fooled again would be too damaging, both to herself and her children.

"Call it what you will," she answered him, grimly resolved on keeping her feet on the ground. "I want protection for my children. Give me that, Keir, and I'll certainly consider you worth having in my life. You can risk it or not, as you please, but I'm not risking anything more."

"The hurt goes so deep," he murmured, his eyes softening with compassion.

It made Rowena squirm inside. But she had nothing to be ashamed of. It wasn't she who had betrayed her commitments. "I didn't ask you to come here," she said resentfully.

"No. Jamie did. He was worried for you. With good reason."

"I'm not a basket case. I can cope. I've done it before and I can do it again."

Though she was hopelessly rusty on her secretarial skills. She would have to do some computer courses to update herself before applying for a job. If that became necessary. She didn't know what the law was on maintenance payments. Phil was seeing a solicitor today. Maybe she should see one, too. At least find out what her position was.

"You don't have to cope this time," Keir said, shrewdly reading her uncertainties. "Just let me do it for you."

How could he be so confident of delivering what Phil had found too oppressive? "You're welcome to try, Keir. But let me tell you, when you really get hit in the face with the difficulties, it can be another story. I'll be more impressed with action," she informed him, her eyes broodingly sceptical.

"Did it ever occur to you to act yourself, Rowena? To let me know you were pregnant?"

The softly spoken challenge sliced through the bank of defences she'd been feeding. It plucked at her heart. There was pain in his eyes, pain she couldn't dismiss.

"If only you'd told me," he went on, such infinite regret in his voice, the pain of loss, all the years he had been deprived of knowing Jamie, the baby years and the wonderful little-boy years, starting school, sports days where Jamie always won his races, the fun and the joy of so many things.

Rowena was suddenly gripped by guilty confusion. She had blamed Keir for not coming back to her, but was the blame all his? What did she know of his life in the years following the accident? The need to justify her own course impelled her to speak.

"I was only seventeen, Keir, and my parents... It was so bad, I was frightened of even mentioning your name, let alone..." She winced at the memory of endlessly fraught days, weeks, months. "And you didn't write to me, didn't let me know."

"I did, Rowena," he asserted quietly.

He'd said that yesterday, too. He could have written, for all she knew. She shook her head in helpless anguish. "You don't understand. Everything to do with you was destroyed. It was like living in a nightmare, and when Mum realised I was pregnant and I had to tell her you were the father, she was so unbalanced—"

"I'm sorry," Keir murmured. "You shouldn't have had to be so alone." He crouched again and gently squeezed her knees. "I'm sorry it was like that for you."

She doubted he could ever imagine what it had been like. No one could. "They wanted me to have an abortion," she stated flatly. "I refused. So they sent me to my aunt in Queensland. It seemed best. I knew you weren't in a position to help me, and I didn't want to add to whatever you were going through. It was all such a mess."

"My parents would have helped."

"I would have been disowned by my parents if I'd gone to them, Keir."

"Yes, of course."

"I thought the only thing to do was to ride it through and wait until you came home. I thought... I believed..."

He grimaced. His eyes begged more belief from her. "There were good reasons I didn't seek you out, Rowena. But I swear to you, if I'd known you'd had my child, nothing would have kept me away. Nothing."

Was it true? He seemed so sincere. Maybe she had judged him unfairly, without enough knowledge of his side. What did he consider good reasons?

"I would have given you and Jamie everything I could," he went on vehemently.

I'll never know that, Rowena thought sadly, *never know what might have happened if I'd somehow got in touch with him.* She didn't want to think about it. It was all too late. "It's pointless going over what might have been, Keir."

"Yes, it is," he agreed, withdrawing his touch and rising again. "And you want proof." He suddenly grinned, his whole face lighting up with pleasurable anticipation. "Action you will have aplenty, Rowena."

She stared at him, forcibly reminded of how attractive he was and how much she had once felt for him. But she wouldn't make the mistake of falling in love with him again. That would only be asking for more heartache. This time she would follow her head, not her heart. He hadn't said what his good reasons were for not seeking her out.

Before she could pursue the point, Jamie came in, carefully balancing a cup of coffee on its saucer. Sarah followed, bearing a plate of cookies. Impossible to continue an intimate conversation in front of the children.

"Are you feeling better, Mum?" Jamie asked anxiously as he set his offering down on the occasional table beside her armchair.

"Yes, thank you, Jamie."

"These are my favourite cookies. You'll like them, Mummy," Sarah encouraged, handing her the plate.

"Thank you, Sarah."

They all proceeded to sit down, Keir in the armchair opposite her, the two children on the lounge. Both Jamie and Keir watched her, waiting for her to eat and drink what had been ordered and brought for her. Sarah studied Keir with keen interest.

At least her younger daughter didn't appear confused or upset by Jamie's identification of Keir as his real father, Rowena observed in some relief. Sarah was clearly consumed with curiosity.

But what about Emily? Rowena worried as she dunked a cookie into her coffee and lifted it quickly to her mouth to satisfy the onlookers. The cat was out of the bag, well and truly. Jamie would hold his tongue if she asked him to, but Sarah couldn't be trusted not to blurt out everything. She was too young to understand tact and discretion.

So much for waiting another day, Rowena thought disconsolately. Now she had to explain about two fathers going missing, and the return of one was not the one Emily would want. Keir would have his work cut out to win her older daughter over to accepting him as a replacement for Phil on any terms whatsoever.

She finished the cookie and took a sip of coffee.

"Are you and Mum friends now?" Jamie asked Keir hopefully.

Rowena almost choked.

"Your mother needs some convincing that I mean what I say, Jamie," Keir answered quietly. "That will take a little time."

"You're not going to give up?" Jamie pressed.

"No. Nothing will make me give up," Keir assured him.

"See?" Jamie said to Sarah, nudging her to take notice.

"Yes," she agreed, gravely nodding her approval at Keir. "A real prince never gives up."

"A prince!" Rowena spluttered over her coffee cup.

Sarah looked at her as though she was slow off the mark. "Jamie said it was like a fairy tale. The wicked witch took Daddy away, so the prince has come to look after us. And he's going to take us to a castle where nothing bad can happen to us."

"Oh, my God!" Rowena groaned, appalled at the licence Jamie had taken in explaining the situation to his little sister.

"I have to show your mother that the castle is hers first, Sarah. That could take a few days," Keir warned indulgently.

"Stop!" Rowena cried, crashing her cup down and standing to take command. "Jamie, take Sarah out to the family room and stay there until I join you. I want a private talk with—with your father. And no more fairy tales. That's an order."

Jamie sighed and stood up, tugging Sarah with him.

"I like fairy tales, Mummy," Sarah protested.

"No more today," Rowena amended.

"Come on, Sarah," Jamie urged. "We'll build a castle with your blocks."

"Yes," Sarah gleefully agreed and skipped along beside him as they exited from the lounge room.

"I like fairy tales, too," Keir remarked, rising from his chair. He gave Rowena a warm smile of approval. "Thank you for calling me Jamie's father. It sounded good."

Rowena found her tongue. "How dare you encourage this—this fantasy when—when...?" She floundered.

"I like your daughter very much," Keir said, still smiling as he moved closer to her.

"You're making trouble for me," she cried in anguished protest.

"Rowena." His arms enfolded her and his eyes glowed with a compelling intensity. "I want a happy ending. The only person who can stop that happening is you. All I ask is that you give it a chance."

"You're deluding yourself."

"Let's see if I am."

"Life isn't like a fairy tale. It's..."

His head was bending towards hers. There was a purposeful glitter in his eyes, a simmering glitter, a mesmerising glitter. Rowena forgot what words she had meant to say. Her mouth remained open.

His lips brushed hers and ignited a field of electric tingles. She gasped. His mouth blanketed the sensitive area, soothing it with a warm pressure that was too captivating to resist. It tugged at memories ... her very first kiss on her sixteenth birthday.

She'd been waiting and waiting for it to be Keir who gave her that first kiss. How she'd longed for it, willing him to see she was grown-up enough for him, and it had been so right, so perfect, the touch like thistledown at first, and then ...

He was doing it now, the slide of his tongue over the sensitive inner tissues of her lips, so tantalising, exciting ... But she shouldn't be letting him do it. He shouldn't be stimulating these feelings. She wasn't sixteen any more. Nor seventeen. Yet there was a need in her to know if it would all be the same as it had been then.

Keir lifted his head, ending the kiss, leaving her mouth aquiver with anticipation. He stroked her cheek with feather-light fingertips. His eyes held a soft tenderness that curled into her heart. "A new start, Rowena," he murmured.

No, that was impossible, her mind dictated. The fantasy of reliving her youth crumbled against the stark force of the realities she had to face. "We can't go back, Keir."

"We can move forward." He smiled. "I'll go now and start the action to prove it."

He was at the doorway to the foyer before she recollected herself enough to say, "You don't appreciate how difficult this will be. There's Emily."

He paused to look back, still smiling. "I look forward to meeting her."

"She's older than Sarah."

"Jamie told me. Don't worry. I'll handle it." He grinned. "I'll fight all your dragons, Rowena. I have a quest."

And on that quixotic note he left. His devil-may-care grin stayed behind, stamped indelibly on Rowena's mind. He didn't know. He didn't understand. He didn't care what barriers he had to jump over or negotiate around. He had a quest.

CHAPTER NINE

"WHAT'S the wicked witch's name?" Emily demanded again.

Rowena sighed. Her careful explanation of the present situation had been completely supplanted by Jamie's fairy tale. Apparently it had more appeal. Children had a habit of judging things in black and white. Greys, Rowena reflected, were probably too difficult a concept to grasp.

"Her name is Adriana Leigh, and I told you, Emily, she's not a wicked witch," Rowena answered with somewhat frayed patience as she bent to kiss her older daughter good night.

"She is so, too, if she took Daddy away," came the petulant reply.

"Your father wanted to go, Emily."

"She put a spell on him," Sarah piped up. "That's what wicked witches do."

It was a fairly apt interpretation of what had happened, Rowena thought, although if it hadn't been Adriana, it would have been someone else sooner or later. Adriana had merely hastened what had been brewing.

"Can we undo the spell, Mummy?" Emily asked hopefully.

Rowena gently stroked her hair. "I'm afraid not, darling. But your daddy did say he'd come and see you."

"When?"

"I guess when he's ready to, Emily."

"For Christmas?"

"I don't know. Perhaps."

"He'd better. Or she is so, too, a wicked witch," Emily declared with conviction.

Rowena could only silently agree. Whatever Phil's faults, Adriana was pandering to them, not caring who got hurt. On the other hand, Adriana's influence didn't exonerate Phil of responsibility for his actions.

She gave Emily an extra good night kiss. "Go to sleep now and don't worry about it. Daddy will call us and let us know. All right?"

"All right, Mummy."

She snuggled obediently into her pillow. Rowena moved to the door, checking that Sarah was still settled. She was well burrowed down, her head barely visible. Yet as Rowena switched off the light, Sarah had the last word.

"Anyhow, we've got the prince on our side, Emily."

A more comforting thought than any she'd been able to give, Rowena conceded ruefully, but if the prince fell down on his quest, the collapse of the fairy tale would cause more trauma than Rowena cared to contemplate. Did Keir even begin to comprehend all the ramifications of what he had put in motion?

Jamie was waiting for her in the kitchen, seated on the counter stool again, his book ostensibly open. "Are you mad at me, Mum?" he asked without preamble.

What he had done was irrevocable. There was no point in recriminations. Besides, perhaps it would turn out for the best. *Give me a chance,* Keir had said. She had no other option now. She forced a smile. "No, I'm not mad at you, Jamie."

His face lit with relief, and a wide grin broke through his cautious control. "The flowers look great, don't they?"

Beyond him, on the coffee table in the family room, sat a glorious basket of flowers, Christmas bells, dark red lilies, scarlet carnations, yellow daisies, a profusion of blooms in season. It had come just after Emily had arrived home from school, and attached to it was a card that read, "To cheer you, Keir."

It had lent substance to the fairy tale.

Rowena had to concede it had also given her heart a lift. It had been years since Phil had given her flowers. "They're beautiful, Jamie. It was nice of Keir to send them," she added warmly, wanting to erase any guilt Jamie might have about going to Keir behind her back.

"He explained about you being separated by the accident and all that. He really does care about us, Mum. I could tell."

"Yes, I think he does," Rowena agreed, wishing she had heard the *all that.* She would like to know Keir's good reasons for not seeking her out when he'd returned to Australia from California. Not that it really mattered now.

A new start. Was he courting her with flowers?

"You won't have to worry about Dad getting nasty on you any more, Mum. Keir said he would fix everything," Jamie said with satisfaction.

Rowena hoped Jamie's faith in his new-found father was well-placed. She couldn't quite quell her fears over what might eventuate now that Keir had thrown his hat in the ring. She frowned over Jamie's use of his Christian name. "I don't think you should call him Keir, Jamie."

"He suggested it. He said it would be easier for Emily and Sarah if we all called him Keir. That way they won't get mixed up about fathers. I thought it was a good idea."

It amazed and impressed Rowena that Keir had been considering the girls' reaction to him even before he met them. It showed he really did care how they felt. "What about you, Jamie? Did you want to call him Dad?"

"No. Not yet anyway. It didn't feel right."

Too soon. Too big a leap in one day. Phil had been his dad for so long, Jamie couldn't be expected to suddenly transfer that identity to a virtual stranger. "How do you feel about Keir?"

Another wide grin. "He passed all my tests, Mum. For my real father, I don't know that I could have got much better."

She had to smile. "Well, I hope he lives up to his test score."

"He's doing good so far."

"Time will tell, Jamie."

Would Keir pass her tests, as well? Rowena wondered. Even her son had been wary of giving his trust. Rejection cast a long shadow.

Caution—that was what was needed. Having been plunged into the wilderness by Phil's defection, it was very tempting for her to be swept along on what might feel like a magic carpet, but she couldn't squash the sense of dangers lurking at the edges, ready to grab them all if she wasn't vigilant.

Rowena's apprehensions, however, received one telling blow the next day. The mail was delivered at ten o'clock, and amongst an assortment of Christmas cards was an official letter from a Chatswood bank. It was not the bank Phil usually dealt with, and it was addressed to her. Mystified, Rowena opened the envelope and read the letter enclosed.

It informed her that trust accounts had been opened in the names of her three children. If she would call at the bank, at her convenience, the paperwork could be completed for her to become the signatory for each account.

Rowena was totally stunned at the speed with which Keir had moved to fulfil her demand. More than her demand. He had not only opened a trust account for Jamie, but for Emily and Sarah, as well. He must have done it straight after he left her yesterday for this letter to have come in the mail this morning.

She reread it to make absolutely sure she wasn't hallucinating. Still she could hardly bring herself to believe it. There was only one way of checking if it was bona fide—go to the bank in question and present it to whomever was in charge of such things.

Emily and Jamie would not be home from their last school day of the year until three-thirty. She had plenty of time to get herself to Chatswood and back. She dressed in her navy suit again, feeling the need to look smart. Sarah was happy to have the opportunity to wear her best dress. It was made of a pretty red and white print, with a white yoke and pockets. Sarah loved red.

The drive from their home in Killarney Heights only took fifteen minutes. Rowena entered the bank with Sarah in tow at eleven forty-five and made her way to the inquiries counter. A young woman came to attend to her needs, and Rowena handed her the letter. "My name is Rowena Goodman and I've come to settle this business," she said, hoping everything was in order.

The woman read the letter then smiled at Rowena. "Would you please take a seat, Mrs. Goodman? I'll check if the bank manager can see you now."

Rowena did as she was told, but her heart pounded with apprehension. Did bank managers oversee new accounts? Her only experience with a bank manager was over a home loan with Phil, and that had involved a lot of money. Phil had only recently finished paying off the mortgage on the house.

A few highly nervous minutes later, the door to a side office opened and a semi-bald, middle-aged man wearing gold-framed spectacles made a beeline for Rowena, his hand already stretched out in greeting. "Mrs. Goodman, delighted to meet you. I'm Harvey Ellis, the manager."

Rowena stood and shook his hand. "How do you do, Mr. Ellis." The letter had to be genuine! She wouldn't be welcomed like this if it wasn't. "This is my daughter Sarah," she offered belatedly.

"Hello, Sarah." His voice dripped with indulgence and he beamed at Sarah as though a three-year-old girl was his idea of a Christmas box.

"Hello," Sarah replied, staring at his shiny, bald pate.

"Come right this way, Mrs. Goodman. We can sit comfortably in my office while you do the necessary signatures. I trust you have identification with you."

"Yes." Her mind whirled. Driver's licence, credit cards... But she had really only come to satisfy her curiosity, to know if Keir had truly done it.

It was a very streamlined executive office. Rowena and Sarah were ushered to comfortable chairs, and Mr. Ellis settled behind his massive desk. Its clean surface made Rowena wonder if any real work was done here. However, there was one folder in front of the bank manager, and he proceeded to open it.

"Now, as you undoubtedly know, Mr. Delahunty has placed one hundred thousand dollars in each of the children's trust accounts. Jamie, Emily and of course—" he smiled benignly "—Sarah."

"One . . ." Rowena shook her head. Her mind was buzzing with astronomical figures. She must have misheard. "I beg your pardon, Mr. Ellis. Would you please run that past me again?"

"Mr. Delahunty . . ."

It was the same the second time. Rowena sat dazed, vaguely aware that the bank manager was explaining her part as signatory for the children, but none of it sank in. Then he was shoving papers at her and offering her a pen. All she could think of was the enormity of what Keir was handing over to her. It was far, far beyond any expectation she'd had of him.

"Mrs. Goodman?" It was a prompt.

"I have to speak to Mr. Delahunty first. This isn't quite what I thought it was," she said distractedly.

Harvey Ellis looked surprised. "Well, if you'd like to use my phone, Mrs. Goodman . . ."

"Yes, please."

He pushed it towards her.

"I need to speak to him privately," Rowena pressed, too embarrassed to reveal the true situation to the bank manager.

"I'll leave you to it," he said obligingly, standing up. "Will ten minutes be enough?"

"Yes. Thank you."

She didn't know if it was or not, but the moment he'd gone she leapt from her chair, snatched up the receiver and feverishly jabbed the numbers for Delahunty's, knowing them off by heart from calling Phil. She was put through to Keir's secretary.

"Good morning. Keir Delahunty's office. How may I help you?" Her welcoming voice instantly conjured up the homely image.

"It's Rowena Goodman. Is it possible for me to speak to Keir, please?"

"One moment, Mrs. Goodman. I'm sure he'll be happy to take your call," came the warm reply.

Rowena wildly wondered if the news of Keir's interest in her and Jamie was all over the building. If so, Phil might...

"Rowena, what can I do for you?"

"Does Phil know about Jamie's visit? And about you coming to me?"

"I haven't told him."

"Your secretary..."

"Everything held in the strictest confidence. Has something happened, Rowena?"

"No, I—I'm at the bank, Keir."

"I hope Harvey Ellis is treating you as he should."

"That's not the point. This—all this money..."

"Educating children is expensive. Over the years—"

"Keir, I can't accept it!"

"It's simply a safeguard against the future."

"But three hundred thous—" She bit down on the last word, remembering belatedly that Sarah had a mind like a sponge. "It's far too much," she said curtly.

"It's ready cash. I changed my will yesterday, making you and the children my beneficiaries. If anything should happen to me—"

"Keir, for heaven's sake!"

"It's protection for you until we're married."

"Married! Keir, I *am* married. I've only been separated from my husband for two and a half days. It'll be a year before a divorce becomes possible. And I'm not going to be rushed into anything!"

"Rowena, you wanted proof of commitment from me," he said gently. "I want to give it to you. I want to give you everything you need."

"I can't say I'll marry you, Keir. I don't know. It mightn't work. There's so much—"

"I promise I won't rush you," he soothed. "All I ask is that you give us a chance. We'll take one step at a time."

"This step is too big."

"No, it's easy, Rowena. Just attach your signature to whatever needs signing. I can afford to give your children financial security, and I choose to do it. Okay?"

"It's... it's madness."

He laughed. "The best kind of madness there is, Rowena. Are you and the children free tomorrow?"

"Yes. Unless..." It was Saturday tomorrow. Phil might want to see the girls.

"Unless what?"

Then again, he might not. He hadn't called. Why should they wait around on his and Adriana's convenience? Phil had forced separate lives upon them. *Let us lead separate lives,* Rowena thought defiantly. Besides, Keir was showing more caring than her husband—her *ex*-husband—had. A lot more!

"It doesn't matter," she declared with determination. "What do you have in mind?"

"A castle."

Rowena suddenly had a vision of ramparts and turrets. "You can't mean that."

"Well, it's really a house. But we can call it a castle. I'd like you to see it. Will ten o'clock suit for me to pick the family up?"

A smile tugged at her mouth. The magic carpet ride was zipping along at supersonic speed, and she really ought to get off and plant her feet firmly on the ground, but she couldn't help feeling fascinated about where it might lead next. "Yes. Ten will be fine," she heard herself say.

"Now do what Harvey says, Rowena. Then you can go home and bask in a sense of security."

No, she couldn't do it, no matter what argument Keir used. She would feel as though he was buying her. Such a huge commitment from him automatically placed a commitment on her, one she wasn't prepared to give at this juncture in her life.

"The gesture is enough, Keir. I really can't take the money from you, but thank you for placing so much value on my children," she said warmly.

"I want you to feel safe."

"It's good of you. I appreciate it very much. And thank you for the flowers. They're lovely."

"My pleasure. Tomorrow at ten."

She smiled. "We'll be ready." She dropped the receiver in its cradle, feeling distinctly light-headed.

"Was that the prince you were talking to, Mummy?" Sarah asked.

"Yes, it was the prince." In a giddy moment of delight that Keir had proved as good as his word, Rowena scooped Sarah from her chair and hoisted her up against her shoulder. "He's going to sweep us off to a castle tomorrow," she told her darling little daughter.

"A real castle?"

Rowena laughed. She hadn't laughed so light-heartedly for a long, long time. It felt good. "Not quite, Sarah. A home. If the home is right, it feels like a castle."

Sarah grinned. "I like the prince."

He was certainly scoring well at the moment, Rowena thought happily.

"If you marry him, you could be a prin-cess, Mummy."

That brought Rowena down to earth with a thump. The talk about marriage had clearly filtered into Sarah's active little brain, and she might blurt it out at the worst possible moment, creating trouble Rowena could well do without.

"We mustn't think about that yet, Sarah. The prince has to do a lot of brave deeds first."

"He said he wouldn't give up," Sarah reminded her.

"Let's wait and see. He might not mean to give up but it's better to wait and see. It might be bad luck to talk about marrying him. We wouldn't want to give him bad luck, would we?"

Sarah gravely shook her head.

Rowena was relieved to have that settled. She hoped. There was always an unpredictable element with Sarah.

The bank manager entered the office. She turned to him with beaming confidence. "Mr. Ellis, thank you so much for your time, but I can't continue with this business right now. Mr. Delahunty will be making further arrangements with you."

"Oh! Well, thank you for coming in, Mrs. Goodman."

He escorted her and Sarah to the bank door, showing them every courtesy. Rowena felt the pleasurable glow of being worth three hundred thousand dollars even though she didn't have it. She also felt good about showing Keir she wasn't out for vengeance.

A new start.

Magic words.

She wasn't going to do anything she didn't want to do, but she saw no harm in giving Keir a chance.

He had earned it.

CHAPTER TEN

KEIR DELAHUNTY finished signing the letters his secretary had brought him and handed her the sheaf of papers.

"Is everything all right?"

He glanced at Fay, surprised by her question. "Are you concerned about any of the letters?"

"No. Horses for courses. You looked so grim. I wondered..." She gave him a rueful smile. "Well, Mrs. Goodman sounded anxious when she called you."

He sighed and leaned back in his chair, brooding over the note of fear in Rowena's voice when she'd asked if Phil knew what had developed over Jamie. Was it fear of losing her home or fear that the door would be shut on any chance of Phil coming back to her? Did she still want him?

"It's not an easy time for her," he said.

Fay gave him her owl look. "It's messy, Keir, with Phil working for you."

"Don't I know it," he agreed, flicking her a derisive look for stating the obvious. "I've been considering what to say to him."

"It'll be blood on the floor," Fay warned.

"Maybe. Maybe not. Either way, I will not have Rowena frightened," he said decisively. "I'm going to straighten Phil out on that point."

"Good for you," Fay approved.

He gave her a wry smile. "Not much gets past you, does it, Fay?"

"Old eagle eye strikes again. If it's not too much of an impertinence . . ." She paused, eyeing him warily.

"Go on."

"Is Mrs. Goodman the reason you haven't married?"

He nodded. He didn't mind Fay knowing. She could be trusted, and in a way, it made his situation less lonely. "I've loved Rowena all my life," he revealed. "But she's been hurt, Fay. Badly hurt. Through no fault of her own."

"It's a hard road when someone's been damaged, Keir," Fay advised softly.

He frowned as he remembered the anguish in Rowena's eyes yesterday, the tests of commitment she had thrown down as a challenge to his caring, her fear of him making more trouble for her and her children.

"Somehow I've got to fix it," he said resolutely.

"I wish you luck." She smiled. "I was impressed with Jamie. Your son?"

"Yes," he acknowledged with pride. "How did you know?"

"Well, he's not exactly a dead ringer in looks, but he gets a set expression on his face that is pure you. When he declared he would wait all day if he had to..." She rolled her eyes.

He grinned, his heart lightening momentarily at the strength of character his son had displayed. "Persistence often pays off."

"I hope it does for you this time," Fay said sympathetically.

His grin turned lopsided. "It won't be for want of trying."

"You do have the boy on your side, Keir. That's a big plus."

"I've got to win Emily."

"Who's Emily?"

"Rowena's older daughter. I haven't met her yet. All going well, I shall tomorrow."

Rowena had agreed to his plan for tomorrow, but Keir didn't feel he could take it for granted. *Unless,* she had said. Unless what? Was she hoping, wanting Phil to call? Would she still accept a reconciliation at this point?

Over my dead body, Keir thought grimly. To his mind, Phil had burnt his boats with his rejection of Jamie. Keir was not about to stand by and watch Rowena hurt any further, either.

He looked at his secretary, who was still hovering, and made his decision. "Call Phil up, Fay. I'll talk to him now. It's best done before the weekend."

"Right!" She nodded agreement then waved a salute as she turned to go. "Battle stations at the ready."

He stood and wandered down his office to the table at the far end. Rowena filled his mind. The way she had accepted his kiss yesterday, the bemused, almost hopeful look on her face as he had left her to start proving himself in her eyes. The attraction *was* still there. He was certain of it. The task was to build on it.

His instincts told him speed was critical to success. He had to block Phil out of her mind, fill it with thoughts of a different, happier, easier future. With him. Fay was right about Jamie being on his side. Keir foresaw no problem with Sarah. She was delightfully open. Emily, at five, could be a stumbling block. He would have to be very alert to Emily's sensitivities.

He was pleased Rowena had refused the money for the children, though he wouldn't have begrudged a cent of it. It showed a softening of her stance against him, a return of some faith in his word. He wanted to tell her about the photograph and how it had been used to crush his hopes and dreams, but he wasn't sure she was ready to believe him yet. What if her parents denied showing him any such thing?

No, it was better to concentrate on a new start. Forget the past. It was gone. Rowena had different needs now, urgent needs, and he had to answer them. First and foremost was protection.

A knock on the door alerted Keir to Phil's arrival. He swung around to face one of the most important diplomatic meetings he'd ever had to deal with. He needed a win-win result to set the ground for the future he wanted.

"Keir, you just caught me. I was on my way out to lunch. Something urgent?" Phil asked, a tense edge to the bluff heartiness he was trying to project.

"Urgent and important. I'm sorry if I've inconvenienced you."

"Not at all. Fire away."

"Take a seat, Phil."

Keir gestured to the chairs on the other side of the table and sat down himself, careful to avoid any suggestion of a superior position. Phil Goodman's pride was very much at stake here. Keir knew he had to set the scene for a man-to-man talk, removing any threat his employer status carried.

This had nothing to do with work. Phil had to be assured of that. He had to be left feeling comfortable, not ill-affected in any way by what Keir planned. In fact, the optimum result would be for Phil to feel advantaged by Keir's stepping into the breach. It would prevent any negative fallout on Rowena.

Highly aware of the thin line he had to tread, Keir waited until Phil relaxed in his chair, then looked him straight in the eye and said, "I had a visit from your son, Jamie, yesterday. He informed me that I was his natural father. He gave me facts to substantiate his claim, and I have no doubt whatsoever that he is my child."

Phil looked stunned. "Jamie came to you?"

"Yes." Keir carefully kept his voice level and matter-of-fact. "I subsequently visited Rowena, who confirmed what Jamie told me. She was, however, extremely shocked and upset by his revelation. She had not intended me to know."

Phil ruminated over that for several moments before asking, "How did Jamie find out?"

"He didn't say. It came as a shock to me."

Phil gave a nervous, derisive laugh. "And to me. I only found out myself the other night."

Time for some judicious ego stroking, Keir thought. As much as he disliked any form of manipulation, he was prepared to use every tactical move he could think of to free Rowena from this man's destructive capabilities.

"Jamie is a fine boy, Phil," he said admiringly. "You've done a great job of bringing him up."

"That's mostly Rowena's doing," he conceded without thought. Then wryly, "She's a good mother."

"You were there for him. And you supported him. I can't thank you enough for that. Rowena and I . . . we were separated by circumstances that I'd rather not go into."

"I understand," Phil put in hastily.

"But things change. As with your marriage. Sometimes a relationship doesn't work out and it's better to part and move on. People grow and want to take different directions. Is that how it is with you, Phil?"

He flushed but manfully replied, "Yes, it is."

"These things happen. No one's fault. But I find myself presented with a situation where a responsibility that should have been mine can very properly and appropriately be taken up by me."

Keir paused. Phil's expression had turned wary, uncertain, as though he sensed he was being pushed into a corner from where there was no exit. Keir pushed.

"*You* have shouldered that responsibility long enough, Phil. Do you mind if I take over Jamie's care and support?"

He looked surprised, relieved. "No, that's fine by me, Keir. He is, after all, your boy."

"Thank you. I feel I've missed out on a good deal of Jamie's life. I want to make up for it."

"Yes. It's a shame you were...well, left out. As I said before, I wasn't aware you were Jamie's father until a couple of nights ago, and I felt I had to respect Rowena's decision not to tell you."

Abrogation of responsibility complete. Keir hid his inner contempt. Although it suited him and it was what he wanted, Phil Goodman's dumping of Jamie stirred an urge to smash his face in. Keir controlled the primitive reaction with some difficulty.

"Yes, after all, Rowena was left holding the baby," he couldn't resist saying, hating the fact that it was true of himself, but it was even more true of the man across the table from him. "I appreciate now that I let her down," he continued, concentrating on the next step. "I want to make up for that, too."

A gleam of speculative interest. "What do you have in mind?" Phil was clearly fishing for what might be in it for him.

"Marriage, if she'll have me." Keir plunged straight in.

Phil's mouth tightened. Anger flared in his eyes. He didn't like it one bit that Rowena might end up winning more than he did.

Keir shifted it to a matter of principle. "It's what I would have done had I known about her pregnancy with Jamie. Even though he's ten years old now, I feel the same way about it."

A nasty little smile tilted one corner of Phil's mouth. "Very noble of you, Keir. I admire you for taking your responsibility so seriously. But man to man, you should get to know Rowena again first before proposing. She expects one hell of a lot from a man."

And how many times did you let her down? Keir thought caustically. "I did know Rowena for a long time," he said, keeping his tone level and matter-of-fact.

"Knowing her and living with her are two different things," Phil said, scoffing.

"I'm prepared to take my chances on that."

"Your problem," was the mocking concession.

Keir's fingers began to clench into a fist. It took an act of will to relax them. For Rowena's sake, he had to remain civilised. It was better that Phil vented his sour grapes on him, where it couldn't hurt. One day, Keir vowed, when he'd won the right to stand by Rowena's side, Phil Goodman would get what was coming to him if he insulted Rowena again.

"Thank you for your advice, Phil," he said, keeping the savage streak at bay. "I take it you don't actually object to my marrying Rowena."

He brooded over the proposition for several moments, not caring for it but having no reasonable grounds for objection. "The girls are mine," he said possessively.

"No question. I respect that, Phil," Keir soothed. "Do you intend to contest custody of them?"

"No." He flushed again. "They're better off with Rowena," he added quickly. "I can't recommend her as an understanding wife—" another spiteful stab "—but she is a good mother."

"I thought she would be."

"Of course, I'll be paying maintenance for Emily and Sarah and I expect reasonable access."

Putting a good face on it, Keir thought cynically. He was tempted to test the depth of Phil's devotion to his daughters. "Should Rowena consent to marry me, Phil, I wouldn't mind supporting them. You've supported Jamie all these years."

"No, no, they're my daughters," he protested. "You didn't know about Jamie."

"I just feel I owe you so much."

"I appreciate that, Keir." He liked it, too. "As you remarked, these things happen."

"They do indeed."

And Keir wouldn't be at all surprised if the maintenance payments and the paternal feeling wilted away as time went on. Especially if Adriana Leigh had her way. That calculating lady didn't have a maternal bone in her body, and she wouldn't take kindly to the money going out instead of coming in.

Rowena was right not to trust her ex-husband. Phil Goodman was looking for ways out. Keir instinctively increased the carrot.

"You're a generous man, Phil. I understand you're leaving Rowena the family home."

"It's for the family," he agreed, then had quick second thoughts. "Though should Rowena remarry and the house is sold, the proceeds of the sale would be divided between us."

"That would certainly happen if I can persuade Rowena to marry me," Keir assured him. "As far as I'm concerned, you could have all the proceeds, but Rowena might feel entitled to half."

Phil's mouth curved into a self-satisfied little smile. "I wish you, luck, Keir. Rowena couldn't do better than you."

"That's big of you." It was worth the pay-off to get him off Rowena's back. "I hope you'll be happy with your decisions. I thought it better to have all this out in the open so everyone knows where they stand."

"Good idea." Warmly approved.

"Well, I won't hold you up from your lunch any longer."

Keir stood and offered his hand. Phil Goodman rose and gripped it.

Deal done.

Keir watched him leave, savagely wishing it was the last he ever had to see of Phil Goodman, but he knew he had to live with his presence for a while. Alienating the man would inevitably rebound on Rowena and her children.

He wondered how Rowena could have been so deceived about the character of the man she had married.

The need to feel loved, he decided. The words she had hurled at him echoed painfully through his mind. *He gave me what you didn't give.*

It ill behove him to forget that. Besides, Phil could look good and sound good, and he *was* good at his job. Keir had chosen to employ him. Rowena had chosen to marry him. But for Phil Goodman, they might never have met again, might never have had a second chance to come together. That was a sobering truth.

Could love rise out of hurt?

Tomorrow, Keir thought. Tomorrow he had to get everything right for Rowena. And give her all that she needed to be given. He must not fail her this time. His second chance was, in all probability, his last chance.

CHAPTER ELEVEN

"HE'S here, Mum!" Jamie's excited voice rang through the house.

Rowena's heart skittered. It was not quite ten o'clock. Keir was five minutes early. Not that it mattered. She was ready. They were all ready. But she couldn't help worrying how Phil was going to react to her involvement with Keir Delahunty. Her ebullient mood of yesterday had wilted overnight.

She heard the front door open, Jamie running out to greet his father. His real father. Whom he had a right to know. Impossible to stop that now.

"Come on, Emily," Sarah urged, her voice high with excitement, too. "The prince is here to take us to the castle."

Rowena winced. She shouldn't have embellished the fairy tale in Sarah's mind. Maybe she was doing everything wrong.

"I'll wait for Mummy."

Sarah dashed through the kitchen to follow Jamie.

Emily hung back, unsure of her place in this new situation.

Rowena picked up her handbag from the counter. Her gaze fell briefly on the large crystal bowl of big black cherries. It had been delivered by taxi yesterday afternoon. From Keir. He had remembered her favourite fruit. Flowers, cherries, the trust accounts, a house... She took a deep, calming breath. It was good to feel valued again, she told herself, even if it was a risky business.

She turned to Emily with an encouraging smile and held out her hand. "Keir is a nice man," she assured her. "You'll like him."

"Will he like me?" Emily asked, trustingly slipping her hand into Rowena's.

Rowena squeezed it lightly. "Of course. He has to or he's not a prince."

That was the truth of it, though Rowena instantly wished she hadn't said it. This fairy tale business had to stop. It was too facile, too fertile a ground for future disillusionment. She didn't want her children subjected to another, possibly worse, disappointment in their young lives. If Keir didn't live up to the expectations he'd raised, how was she going to explain it all away, compensate?

As she and Emily stepped onto the front porch, he was coming up the path with Jamie and Sarah dancing around him. He was wearing blue jeans and a red T-shirt, and Rowena was instantly struck by a sense of déjà vu, Keir as a university student in happier times, coming to collect Brett for a football game or a cricket match, her at her parents' front door, waiting to ask if she could tag along, too.

He smiled as he saw her, just as he always had, and her heart turned over. Keir... Then Jamie's and Sarah's voices reminded her that time hadn't slipped back, and the years of separation from that age of innocence made their former relationship irrecoverable. Emily's little hand gripped hers more tightly. It rammed home that the past was gone.

"Good morning," Keir greeted them warmly, his gaze sweeping from her to the little girl hugging her side.

"Hello, Keir," Rowena returned as naturally as she could. "This is my daughter Emily."

"I'm happy to meet you, Emily." He crouched to be more her height. "What lovely blue eyes you have!"

"They're like my daddy's."

"So they are."

"Do you know my daddy?"

Rowena tensed. Emily was clearly fixated on her father and holding Keir at a distance.

Keir gave her a reassuring smile. "Yes, I know him. He works with me." The open establishment of a link made him less of a stranger.

"I've got green eyes like Mummy," Sarah piped up.

"I noticed that, Sarah. They're lovely, too," Keir assured her.

"Your hair is the same as Jamie's," Emily said, stepping forward to touch the cowlick at his left temple.

Keir laughed. "Well, I guess we've all got a bit of everyone. That's what families are like."

"Yes, they are," Emily agreed, pleased at having found a familiarity that made Keir properly acceptable.

Rowena's inner tension eased. The initial awkwardness with Emily had been smoothed, and Keir had managed to end it on a positive note.

He straightened to include Jamie in the group. "Now what I need to know is can you all swim?"

"Mum and I can but the girls can't," Jamie informed him.

"Aren't we going to the castle?" Sarah demanded.

"We most certainly are, but the castle has a moat."

"Keir," Rowena reproved.

"I mean the house has a swimming pool," he swiftly corrected, but the whimsy was still there as he added, "It doesn't matter if you can't swim because we can float across it on a raft, but you will need swimming costumes. Have you got some?"

"Yes," they all shouted and dived into the house, Emily as eager as the other two.

"You look breathtakingly beautiful in green," Keir said softly.

It caught Rowena off guard. She flushed. The emerald-green linen skirt with gingham trim on its pockets, teamed with a white T-shirt and a matching green overblouse, was the kind of smart-casual outfit she had thought suitable for today's outing. She hadn't expected a compliment, hadn't anticipated the warm male appreciation in Keir's eyes. It made her feel nervous, unprepared.

"I thought we were looking at a house," she said.

"We are. I own it, so we can do as we please. If you and the children like it, it's yours."

Just like that! Speechless, Rowena searched his eyes and found nothing but steady conviction. "I didn't mean it," she said in helpless agitation. "Not really."

"I do."

He was serious. Deadly serious. Rowena flailed around for an adequate explanation for the way she had behaved, the wild demands she had made. "It felt like everything was crashing around me, Keir. And Phil..."

"I've spoken to Phil. You have nothing to worry about, Rowena. He accepts that I'm seeing you and the children. He sees quite a lot of advantages to him if you marry me."

"You told Phil you were going to marry me?" Rowena squeaked. Keir was moving too far, too fast.

"I informed him it was what I wanted."

"What about what *I* want?" Her mind whirled chaotically around the image of Phil happily shifting all his responsibilities over to Keir, not only Jamie but... "Our home. He'll sell it up."

"I'll provide you with another home, Rowena."

The affirmation of his seriousness threw her into total panic. "But that ties me to you, Keir, and I'm not ready to make such a huge decision. You can't expect it of me. We...it's been so long and...and there's the children..."

"Rowena, you're tied to me anyway. Through Jamie," he stated quietly.

That was true. She steadied for a moment. That was unavoidably true. And she could no longer count on Phil for anything. He had undoubtedly passed the buck to Keir. But *she* was not going to be passed to him. Keir had better believe that.

Her eyes flashed a fierce autonomy. "Don't take me for granted, Keir."

"I don't. I never will," he replied gently.

The soft, caring expression in his eyes reduced her insides to mush. A deep yearning welled up, making her chest ache. A passionate cry filled her mind. *Please let it be true. Please...*

"What about towels?" Jamie called out.

"No need," Keir called back, not missing a beat.

The immediate practicalities of the present snapped Rowena out of the thrall of emotional need. She had to be wary of a rebound effect from Phil's desertion. She had to take stock, be sensible, not surrender to the weakness of leaning on Keir just because he was here and offering her all his strength. How could she know it wouldn't be a mistake that she'd rue as time went on?

"Rowena, why not relax and simply enjoy the day?" Keir suggested quietly. "There'll be no pressure from me. Not for anything."

"Promise?" It sounded hopelessly childish, the kind of thing she'd said to him in their teens when she'd desperately wanted him to grant her a favour.

He grinned. "Promise."

Did he remember, too? His grin was like a burst of sunshine, warming her with the happy beams of the past, making her feel like a teenager again. And this was their first date, just Keir and her, without Brett ... without Phil.

The children broke the dreamy bubble, rushing out of the house, urging her to get her swimming costume so they could go. As she went to collect it, she told herself very sternly to keep her feet firmly planted on the ground. Keir had always been attractive to her. He still was. But that didn't mean everything in the garden was rosy.

She automatically stuffed her costume, a comb and sunblock cream in a beach bag while she tried to calculate the dangerous pitfalls in Keir's plan. She would lose her independence if she accepted Keir's house.

It was different with this home. She felt she had earned half of it over her years of marriage to Phil, and he owed the rest of it to their daughters. It was his choice as much as hers to have a family, and he shouldn't be able to slide out of it now.

It offended Rowena's sense of justice.

No doubt Adriana would profit by it, too, and that scraped raw wounds. What had the wicked witch ever done to deserve to pick up the fruits of Rowena's hard work? *Love Phil as he wanted to be loved,* came the sobering answer.

Rowena sighed away the pain of it. She had to stop thinking of Adriana as the wicked witch. If Phil hadn't wanted Adriana, nothing would have happened. The plain truth was Phil regarded her as the wrong woman for him, and he had certainly proved the wrong man for her.

Better to concentrate on Keir.

He was definitely going too fast for her. She didn't want to reject him, but she did want to slow him down as far as big commitments were concerned. It was important for her to have time to sort herself out and figure out her best future course.

It was an easy matter not to like his house, she decided. There was sure to be something wrong with it, unsuitable for the children, too small a kitchen, a shower stall instead of a proper bath. That was enough to stop Keir from putting the property in her name, which he might be mad enough to do. The experience with the trust accounts demonstrated he was not fooling around.

Satisfied she had wrested back some control of her life, Rowena emerged from the house to find the children already packed into the back seat of Keir's BMW. Keir was standing by the open front passenger door, waiting for her. Rowena's heart skittered again as she locked the door of the house that represented her marriage to Phil Goodman. Somehow it seemed fateful.

CHAPTER TWELVE

ROWENA *loved* Keir's house.

Set on a battleaxe block of land and overlooking a nature reserve leading down to Lane
Cove River, it was constructed in a widened
U shape to take full advantage of the view. The
high central section made an impressive entrance, with tall columns flanking the front
doors. Rowena was fascinated by the graduation
of roof levels that ran down the two wings of the
house. The entire roofline was suggestive of a
phalanx of birds rising up to the sky. She knew
intuitively that Keir had designed it.

"It's big," Jamie commented.

"Castles are always big," Sarah said
authoritatively.

"Will we get lost in it?" Emily asked, her in-
security showing.

"No," Keir assured her with a warm smile.
"Once you see how it's planned inside, you'll
know how easy it is to get where you want to go,
Emily."

They entered a spacious foyer backed by a wall
of panelled Western red cedar. Dominating it was
a breathtaking Pro Hart landscape, spotlighted
for immediate impact. Keir ushered them to the
right, where a gallery overlooked a wonderful,

homey living area, leather lounges, television set, a log fireplace, thick fluffy mats on the slate floor, a breakfast setting in front of glass doors that opened onto an extensive sundeck, and behind the foyer wall a state-of-the-art kitchen and pantry, which left absolutely nothing to be desired.

"This is the heart of the house, Emily," Keir explained. "You start here and always come back to here. Now if we go farther along the gallery we come to the bedroom wing."

There were four bedrooms, two with private ensuites and two sharing a bathroom that had both bath and shower facilities. The master bedroom featured a walk-in wardrobe, and the cupboard space in the other rooms was more than ample. The wing also contained a laundry with every convenience, a boxroom for extra storage and a private study with a computer, photo-copier and fax machine.

Jamie's eyes lit up at seeing the computer. "Do you play games on it, Keir?" he asked eagerly.

"No. But we can soon buy some, Jamie," came the obliging reply.

"Great!"

A father-and-son activity was cemented. It was just what Jamie needed, Rowena thought, and becoming familiar with computers also had to help with his education for today's world. Whatever else happened, it was good, for Jamie's sake, that he had gone to Keir.

Rowena could find nothing to criticise. It would be very easy to be seduced by Keir's castle, she reflected, as he led them to its heart and then down the left wing. A powder room off the foyer was followed by the formal dining room and lounge. Both had a casual elegance that pleased the eye without being intimidating.

The pièce de résistance was the completely enclosed pool and spa room, which also had a bar, a change room with piles of towels and an adjoining shower and toilet. Comfortable cane furniture was spread around for easy entertaining. The entire area was roofed with fibreglass shingles to let in the sunlight. The walls were mainly of glass bricks, and a profusion of ferns and exotic plants gave it a wonderful, tropical atmosphere.

Keir had every conceivable safety aid ready for the children, floaties to go on the girls' arms to make them unsinkable, inflated tyres and rafts. Simply for fun he also supplied a water polo ball and plastic ducks and boats. The children were wild to instantly try out "the moat," clamouring to get changed as fast as possible. Which, of course, meant Rowena and Keir getting changed, too.

Rowena suffered some initial disquiet at seeing Keir nearly naked in his brief, black swimming costume. The sheer male beauty of his body had always had the power to set her hormones racing, and it was disconcerting to find it was no different now. It made her acutely aware of her own body, clad only in a sleek yellow maillot, but the self-consciousness gradually eased under Keir's relaxed and friendly manner.

The water was heated to a lukewarm temperature. It invited swimming. With no initial chill factor to overcome, it made slipping into the water a real pleasure. Keir helped with the girls, laughing and playing with them, teaching them how to move their arms and legs to propel themselves around the pool. They were soon confident of manoeuvring themselves to wherever they wanted to go. Jamie teased them into being braver.

"This is marvellous, Keir," Rowena happily enthused as she watched the girls frolic like born waterbabies with Jamie pretending to be a submarine. "What made you think of an indoor pool?"

They were sitting on the steps that led into the water, ready to go to the rescue if needed.

She turned to him quite naturally, appealing for the answer that hadn't come. "I don't remember swimming being a passion for you."

His smile held a touch of irony. "I guess it became a habit. The kind of injuries I had led to a lot of hydrotherapy. And swimming was the best exercise for strengthening my leg muscles again."

She had noticed the faded but still discernible scars on his legs and wondered how many operations it had taken to put everything right. It had been a long time since she had considered how much pain he had suffered, not only physical but emotional, as well.

"What was in the letter you wrote me, Keir?" she asked, suddenly impelled to know, to understand what he had felt in those sad, broken months following Brett's death.

He grimaced.

"You don't have to tell me if you don't want," she said quickly, realising she had contravened the new-start agreement and not really wanting to dredge through the past again. It wasn't fair, after all this time. People did change. She had changed. Probably for the worse, she thought ruefully.

"I wanted to know how you were," he answered slowly, as though feeling for the words. He scooped up a handful of water and watched it trickle through his fingers. "I knew Brett's death would have hit you hard," he continued. "The shock and the grief, the sudden empty hole in your life. It worried me...how you were coping. With everything."

With him gone, as well? Had he any idea how much she had missed him? He lifted his gaze to meet hers, and the deep, dark regret in his eyes made her heart miss a beat. It also convinced her he spoke the truth as he went on.

"It worried me that I hadn't used any protection on New Year's Eve. I hadn't planned what happened between us that night, Rowena. You were simply irresistible to me. Afterwards... Well, I asked you in the letter if you'd fallen pregnant. And to contact me immediately if you were."

"What would you have done if I had?" she asked, glad he had thought of the risk they'd taken and the possible consequences.

"Got my parents to fly you to the States so we could plan what was best for you."

"No marriage?" she mocked lightly, disappointed with the answer.

"I didn't think it would be right to tie you to me in the circumstances, Rowena," he said softly. "It was more likely than not that I'd be crippled for life."

"Oh!" She turned away as she felt the hot burn of a flush race up her neck. He had been thinking of marriage, but caring more about *her* future.

"I also wrote, if you weren't pregnant to get on with your life, go to university as you'd planned and do your arts course. Since it might be a very long wait before I could come back to you, I said to feel free about going out with other guys and having fun. I wanted you to enjoy all there was to enjoy because that was what being young was for, exploring life and finding out what you really wanted."

"Didn't you believe I wanted you?" she asked in a very small voice, wishing she had never started this conversation.

"Rowena, I didn't want you to waste the years if I could never walk again."

"And that's why there was only one letter," she said sadly. "You set me free."

"I thought I'd done that, yes."

She had to know it all now, had to know the truth. "How long did it take for you to walk again?"

"Eighteen months. I worked very hard at it so I could come back to you."

"Then why didn't you?" She turned to him with anguished eyes. "What were the good reasons, Keir?"

"Rowena..." He didn't want to tell her. She could see the reluctance, the uncertainty over her reaction. Then he took a deep breath and said, "Your parents..."

"Go on," she urged.

His eyes focused intensely on hers, willing her to listen and accept what he said. "They showed me a photograph of you with a baby in your lap. There was a man crouched beside you. They said you were married, Rowena."

Her heart stopped. She had the numb sense of totally suspended animation. Her mind floated back, and she could see it—the terrible turning point in her life, Keir's life, that her parents had forced upon them in their bitter vendetta against Keir, the photograph she had sent them in the hope of healing the rift with the gift of their grandchild. And it was her cousin, Aunty Bet's son, who had been squatting beside her, playing with Jamie's toes to make him smile. She could see it all. And then her mind shattered under the dreadful enormity of what had been done to them.

The lie—not Keir's, her parents'. And she had accused him, blamed him, rejected him out of hand for dismissing her from his life. The awful injustice of her behaviour towards him rushed in on her. And still she hadn't killed his feeling for her. She couldn't bear the shame of it, the guilt. Tears spurted into her eyes.

"I'm sorry. I'm sorry," she gulped, then turned and fled into the pool, swimming hard, thrashing the water with her arms and legs, her chest hurting with so much pent-up feeling, her heart bleeding from all the might-have-beens.

She reached the other end of the pool. There was nowhere to go, nowhere to hide. She clutched the ledge just below the water level and tried to catch her breath. The water erupted around her as Keir's head and shoulders emerged from it.

"Mummy won!" she heard Sarah crow.

"Keir gave her a good start," Jamie pointed out.

"But Mummy won," Emily said with pride.

Rowena felt proud of nothing. She hadn't won. Too much had been lost.

"It's not your fault," Keir said in a low, intense voice.

She looked at him with agonised eyes. "But I said... I thought..."

"It's not your fault, Rowena. It was your parents' doing. And they're probably not going to like any reconciliation between us, either."

"They're dead."

"How? When?" He looked concerned.

"My father said my mother died of a broken heart. That was when Emily was one. My father then proceeded to drown his sorrows and his liver. He died last year."

"I'm sorry."

"I'm not. I'm glad they're dead," she said savagely. "I'd never forgive them if they were alive. They had no right to interfere so ... so—"

"They were hurting," Keir cut in quietly. "Some people can't ever put the hurt behind them, Rowena. If you can't forgive them, you'll never be able to put it aside and move on, either."

How could he be so understanding when ...?

"They're beyond hurting now," he softly pointed out. "Let it go, Rowena. Let it all go. We can make a new start."

"Can we? Can we really, Keir?" She felt as though her life was a total mess.

"Just give us time, Rowena. You'll see."

He was so sure, so confident, it eased some of the sick churning inside her. If he could forgive and forget, maybe she could, too.

But the sense of having been cheated of the life she should have had remained with her, and it was difficult to maintain a facade of good humour for the children, who were unaware of what had transpired between Keir and herself.

The excitement and exercise in the pool soon made them hungry. They changed into their dry clothes and Keir led them out to the sundeck in front of the kitchen where he barbecued sausages, which he served with an array of tempting salads and crispy bread rolls. This was followed by ice cream, scooped into cones for easy licking. It was a relaxed and happy family luncheon, thoroughly enjoyed by the children. Even Emily's blue eyes sparkled at Keir.

He should have been their father, not just Jamie's, Rowena couldn't help thinking. She was haunted by the words Keir had thrown at her. *Is it my fault that the woman I loved married someone else? That the children I wanted with her are Phil Goodman's?* Would he ever be able to forget the girls were Phil's and treat them as his own?

He was good with them. Would he always be?

She felt a fierce love for her daughters. Even though Phil was their father, they were very much part of her. Keir had said that, too. Maybe he could put aside the fact they'd been fathered by another man. On the other hand, Phil had seemed to do so with Jamie, but when it had come to the crunch...

But Keir was different to Phil. It wasn't fair to judge him by another man's failings. Despite the passage of all these years, Keir remained steady in his love for her. Or was he clinging to a dream that had been lost a long time ago?

Time. Time would tell. She had told Jamie that.

"I wish I could swim like Jamie," Emily said with a wistful sigh.

"Would you like me to teach you?" Keir offered.

"Can you?" Her eyes lit with hope.

"Well, I taught your mother when she was a little girl."

"Did he, Mummy?"

"Yes, he did, Emily." How she had adored him, even as a little girl. He had been kinder and far more patient with her than her brother, Brett.

"Can you teach me now? This afternoon?" Emily pressed.

"We could have your first lesson. It might take a few before you take off like a mermaid," Keir warned.

Emily giggled. "Mermaids have tails, Keir."

"Legs are probably better," he returned with a grin.

He hadn't lost his giving nature, Rowena thought warmly.

They cleaned away the luncheon dishes and returned to the pool. Sarah was flagging, ready for her afternoon nap. She was happy to curl up on one of the cane lounges and watch Emily's swimming lesson. Rowena sat with her. Jamie elected to help Keir by showing Emily how to follow his instructions. Learning how to float was the first step, and Keir quickly earned her trust.

"Is teaching Emily how to swim a brave deed, Mummy?" Sarah whispered.

Rowena had to smile. "Yes, it is, Sarah."

"The prince will do it," came the vote of confidence. Demonstrating her complete trust in him, Sarah closed her eyes, gave a contented little sigh and went to sleep.

By the end of the day, Rowena had to acknowledge that Keir had done a great deal towards gaining both acceptance and real liking from her three children. After Emily's swimming lesson and Sarah's nap, he put on a video of Walt Disney's *Aladdin*, which was greatly enjoyed. For their evening meal he took them to a McDonald's, always considered a treat.

When they arrived home, the girls clamoured for him to stay and tell them a bedside story about when Mummy was a little girl. Then Jamie wanted to discuss the merits of the computer games in the catalogue Keir had found and given him. As a new-family-togetherness day, it had to be counted as highly successful.

But it was only one day, Rowena told herself, not wanting to build too many hopes on it. Nevertheless, she deeply appreciated all the effort Keir had put into giving joy and pleasure. The children had been wonderfully distracted from the misery Phil's desertion could have brought.

Rowena tried to examine her own feelings. She could not deny the underlying yearning for the fulfilment of her youthful dreams, yet the break-up with Phil had eroded her confidence in being able to live up to Keir's expectations. What if she fell short? What if the rightness she felt with him was simply a desire to feel it because she was frightened of standing alone? It was a scary world for someone who had been out of the work force as long as she had.

"Jamie said to tell you good night." Keir's voice broke into her private reverie. "I've put his light out."

She swung around from the laundry tub where she had been rinsing swimming costumes. "Thank you, Keir. For everything," she added in a rush of gratitude for his being the man he was.

"Would you like me to go now?" he asked quietly.

"No, I..." Was it wise to be alone with him when she was feeling so...needful? He stood in the doorway, almost filling it—big, solid, strong—and the urge to step forward and lean on him, to feel his arms enfold her with the promise of holding her safe forever, coursed through Rowena with close to irresistible force. "Would you like a cup of coffee?" she blurted.

He smiled. "Very much."

His smile curled around her heart, squeezing it tight. It was the smile of the Keir she had loved, who had loved her. There was a dull ache in her stomach, a faint quiver in her thighs. It shocked her into action.

I'm playing with fire, she thought, as she hurried ahead of him to the kitchen. It was wrong to want another man when she was still married to Phil. But Phil had Adriana. Why should she care what he thought, what anyone thought? Who cared about her? Only Keir.

And the children, she sternly corrected herself. She had to remember the children.

She was reaching for the electric jug when the wall phone above it rang. She grabbed the receiver as though it was a lifeline out of her internal churning. "Hello. Rowena Goodman speaking," she said, turning to wave Keir to one of the armchairs in the family room. It was sensible to establish space between them.

"Well, it's about time you were home," a voice drawled in her ear.

The tempting excitement of a moment ago drained into a sick hollowness.

It was Phil.

CHAPTER THIRTEEN

GUILT at having been out all day was swiftly dissipated by a strong surge of self-determination. Why should she be at Phil's beck and call? He had chosen to be with Adriana. He couldn't expect the wife he had scorned to dance attendance on him, as well. Any meeting they had should be by mutual consent, with consideration given to both sides.

"I'm home now, Phil," she stated, her tone deliberately neutral.

Keir froze midway from the kitchen to the family room. His gaze swung sharply to her, assessing her reaction to the call. She had the sense of something fiercely primitive emanating from him, as though he were a warrior of old, poised to do battle to protect his territory.

"I suppose you've been with Keir Delahunty," Phil said snidely.

Rowena felt her face tighten. No doubt Phil would like to justify his actions by putting her involvement with Keir on the same level as his with Adriana. She would not give him that exoneration.

"What do you want to talk to me about?"

He laughed. "No need to get your knickers in a twist, Rowena. I know what's going on."

He made it sound dirty, and it wasn't. She had nothing to be ashamed of. "Is there some purpose to this call?" she demanded coldly.

"I came to visit the girls this afternoon."

Guilt struck again. Rowena stubbornly repelled it. Phil could have given her fair warning. "I'm sorry your trip was wasted. If you'd—"

"Oh, it wasn't wasted. I picked up all my things. Our bedroom is now completely yours."

A chill ran down her spine at the thought of Phil coming in and removing all his personal possessions from their home. It was such a final act. Seven years...gone. And she hadn't even been here to witness it. Maybe it was easier that way, but it seemed underhand, like a thief in the night.

"I see," she said tightly. "Thank you for letting me know it wasn't burglary."

"Don't tell me you were about to ring the cops."

"No. I haven't been in our—my—bedroom since coming home."

"Busy with the kids, I take it," he said sardonically.

Conscious of Emily's need to see her daddy, Rowena smothered her resentment at his mockery of proper parenting and said, "We'll be home tomorrow if you want to visit the children."

"I have other plans for tomorrow."

Not so much as a pause to reconsider, Rowena thought. It was typical of his self-centred attitude. "Then could we make an arrangement so they don't miss you next time?'' she pressed, wanting something definite so she could organise herself accordingly.

"Well, as you pointed out, Christmas is coming up next week. I'll take the girls out for a while on Christmas morning, get them out of your hair while you're cooking the turkey."

No mention of Jamie. Rowena instantly resolved to invite Keir for Christmas Day. She would not have Jamie left out of having a father. "I presume you won't be staying for the turkey."

"No. Adriana and I are booked in at a hotel for their festive spread."

No work for Adriana. Not that Rowena cared about that. She would much prefer to have a family Christmas in her home than go to a hotel where the children wouldn't feel at ease. "What time should we expect you?'' she asked.

"Oh, ten-thirty, eleven o'clock, whatever," he answered carelessly.

She wanted to say, *Don't bother,* but she held her tongue, mindful that it wasn't only her feelings to be considered. "You will come, won't you, Phil? I don't want to tell the girls if they might be disappointed."

"I said I'll be there. You can have the girls waiting for me."

Rowena burned. Had they always danced at Phil's convenience? Looking back, she could see they had, for the most part. As the breadwinner, Phil expected it, and she had thought he deserved the extra consideration. She had tried so hard to be a good wife to him.

"By the way, I've taken the stereo from the lounge, and my favourite CDs."

She frowned, wishing he hadn't done it while she was away, but she didn't begrudge him his precious sound system. It did surprise her he'd been able to fit so much equipment into his Mazda convertible.

"And Adriana took a few bits and pieces she liked."

Adriana? She'd been with him, picking over the corpse of their marriage for what she could get out of it? Snooping through personal possessions, ransacking the house while no one was here to watch over anything? No doubt she had brought her car, too, to carry off the spoils.

Outrage billowed through Rowena, making her heart thump hard and her head pound with the hurtful injury of having her privacy wantonly invaded by a woman who had already taken her husband.

"You invited Adriana into my home?" She barely found voice enough to ask the question.

Phil snorted. "Don't tell me Keir Delahunty hasn't been there."

It wasn't the same. Not the same at all. "What bits and pieces did she take?"

"Nothing I didn't buy, Rowena. You're not entitled to everything, you know."

"I am entitled to be consulted, Phil. Please keep that in mind, or I shall call the police if anything more is taken without my knowledge or consent.''

She was shaking. She fumbled the receiver onto its wall bracket, unsure what her rights were but too upset to argue the point. She would have to see a solicitor. She would have to...

"Rowena," Keir called softly, "if there's anything I can do..."

She stared blankly at him, too caught up in the tatters of her marriage to consider what he was saying. The need to know the worst impelled her feet forward, faster, faster, down the hall to the lounge. Open the door. Light on. The far end of the room bare without the stereo equipment. The china cabinet emptied of the crystal wineglasses, the Capo Di Monte figurine of the card players gone from its pride of place on top of the cabinet. Her gaze swung to the—no, no, not the lamp, too. Not the beautiful wisteria lamp he had bought her for their first wedding anniversary.

Tears welled into her eyes. An arm curled around her shoulders and turned her to a broad chest. She sagged against it, needing comfort, needing a solidity that wouldn't be stolen away from her. "Why?" she cried brokenly. "It was good once. Couldn't he leave it like that, Keir? Does it all have to be destroyed?"

"No. It shouldn't be," he murmured.

"He brought her here," she sobbed. "He let her take my lamp. I was pregnant with Emily when he gave me that. How could he? How could he?"

"I don't know."

"It's like my parents, getting rid of everything to do with you. It was so awful. Like murdering the memories."

"But I'm not gone, Rowena. I'm here with you now," he soothed. "And we'll never be parted again."

"Oh, Keir!" She burst into uncontrollable weeping.

He held her tight and stroked her hair. "I'm sorry I can't wipe all the hurt away. I wish I could."

"Not your fault," she sobbed.

"It's not your fault either, Rowena. You always did your best at everything you undertook. Don't think you're any less of the beautiful person you are because of this. Phil is the lesser person, not you."

"Why is Mum crying?"

Jamie! She'd promised him not to cry. She struggled to control the tears.

"There was a lamp. It's gone," Keir answered.

"So's the stereo. And the—" A hiss of breath. "Did Dad take them?"

"He was here with his friend while we were out. It could have been his friend who took some of the things," Keir added in mitigation. "Jamie, could you bring your mother a box of tissues, please?"

"Sure."

He was back in a trice, and Keir gave Rowena a handful of tissues to mop up her face.

"I'm sorry, Jamie," she choked out. "You can go back to bed now. I'm all right."

"I don't think so," Keir said gravely. "Jamie, can you get the girls up? Your mother is too upset to stay here. I think we should go back to my house tonight."

"No...no, I can't," Rowena protested, afraid of where that might lead and too wrought up to handle any decisions properly.

"It's okay, Mum. Keir will look after you," Jamie assured her. "I'll get Emily and Sarah."

He raced off again.

"Keir," Rowena appealed desperately.

"I can't leave you here, Rowena. Everywhere you turn you'll feel a sense of violation. It's better that you all come with me."

"But..."

"Don't worry. You'll have a bedroom to yourself. One that Phil and Adriana haven't been in."

She shuddered. Would they have? In the light of what had happened, anything was possible.

"You left your bag and keys in the kitchen, didn't you?"

"Yes."

"Come on. We'll collect them and get on our way."

He kept her hugged warmly to his side as they walked to the kitchen. Rowena couldn't think in any coherent fashion. There were too many mixed-up emotions running rampant. With all the upheaval and revelations of the past week, she felt her life had been turned upside down and inside out, and nothing made any sense any more.

When they returned to the hall, her three children were standing in the open doorway to the lounge, staring at the empty spaces.

"See?" said Jamie.

"I bet the wicked witch did it," Emily declared, trying to be loyal to her father.

Sarah turned to Keir. "Can the wicked witch get into the castle?"

"No. I guard the gate, Sarah. You'll be absolutely safe there," he promised.

"It's good to have a brave prince, isn't it, Mummy?"

"Yes," Rowena said weakly, too drained to take anyone to task over the fairy tale.

"Let's go," Jamie urged, leading the way.

Keir took charge of everything. He switched off lights, locked the house, settled Rowena in the front passenger seat of his car and made sure the children had their safety belts fastened in the back seat before taking his place on the driver's side.

Rowena stared at the darkened house as he started the car. It looked abandoned, empty, empty of love and commitment, dead to any happy future. The car moved onto the street and accelerated away. Keir's hand reached across and grasped hers, enveloping it in warmth, linking her to him.

"Trust me, Rowena," he said softly.

A brave prince, she thought. *Brave to take me on, and all the baggage I bring with me.*

She looked at their hands, feeling the strength of his seep into her veins. A helping hand, a loving hand, a hand she could hold onto. It wouldn't slip away from her, would it?

Trust me.

But could she trust herself to do right by him? She was no longer sure what *right* was. Only that Keir's hand felt right in hers. Was that enough on which to let the past go and forge a future together?

CHAPTER FOURTEEN

THE children had fallen asleep without any problem. Keir wasn't worried about them. He was confident of answering their needs and concerns as they arose. There was a wonderful simplicity about children.

He could see Rowena in all three of them, even Emily, trying her best to learn how to swim. It was easy to love them, to give them the attention that made them feel happy within themselves, knowing they had their special place in the affections of the people who counted most in their lives.

Rowena's parents had robbed her of that precious feeling. They had let Brett's death overshadow everything. She hadn't counted any more. Phil had just done the same thing to her. It was like crushing out of her all the value she had as a person, and it was so wrong, so hurtful. It was fortunate that Phil Goodman wasn't within striking distance, because the violence Keir felt towards him was close to murderous.

At least Rowena now knew he hadn't dismissed her, too. He hoped she was beginning to realise how meaningful she was to him. He desperately wanted to heal her hurts, to give her the love and life she deserved. He had to pull her through this, win her trust, give her back the bubbling joy that had once been naturally hers.

He paused by her door to listen again, worrying about her state of mind. The shower in the ensuite had been running for the past half hour. It was a relief not to hear it. He hadn't known whether it was a lethargy of mind and spirit that had kept her standing under the beat of the spray, or some sense of wanting to wash away the rotten distaste of what Phil and Adriana had done.

Whatever . . . it had stopped now. He had given her one of his soft, cotton T-shirts to wear to bed. Maybe she was already settled for the night, but he doubted that sleep would come easily. He remembered a habitual nightly routine from her childhood, and headed for the kitchen.

A mug of hot Milo. It didn't matter if it was no longer a habit with her. It would recall happier times. He tipped two heaped spoonfuls of the sweet chocolate grains into a mug, poured in milk, stirred the mixture vigorously and slid it into the microwave for two minutes.

Happier times . . .

There had been several little occurrences today when he had felt they had been recaptured, if only fleetingly. This morning . . . Rowena waiting for him on the front porch as he walked up the path to her. When she had appeared in her swimming costume and looked at him in his, barriers had slipped away momentarily, he was sure of it. Then tonight, in the laundry, that vibrant moment when he sensed her wanting to reach out to him, wanting to try what he offered.

If Phil hadn't phoned...

But Phil's crass insensitivity had resulted in Rowena coming here, under his protection. That was a plus. If he could persuade her to stay, it would give him his best chance to show her how it could be for them. They had so many years to make up. He didn't want a second of this new start wasted, didn't want a second of the rest of their future wasted. If only she could see it as he did.

The microwave clicked off. He took out the steaming hot mug, stirred the Milo through the milk again, then, hoping Rowena would welcome it, returned to her bedroom door and knocked.

"Yes?" Definitely awake.

"It's Keir. I've got some hot Milo for you. It might help you sleep."

"Hang on till I put the bedside light on," she called.

He waited, wondering if this was such a good idea after all. It might help Rowena sleep, but seeing her in bed was bound to arouse thoughts and feelings that would make sleep difficult for him. He wanted her so much it was almost a constant ache inside him.

"It's okay. You can come in now."

Think of her as the child she had once been, he sternly advised himself. He had waited years for her to grow into a young woman. He could wait...please, God, not years again.

He left the door ajar to assure her he had no desirous intent. It was important she feel safe with him. Absolutely safe. She was sitting up, propped against the pillows. She looked like a lost waif, the sleeves of his T-shirt dangling shapelessly around her elbows, her black hair in damp wisps around her wan face.

"Are you okay?" he asked.

"More or less." She managed an ironic little smile. "Thanks, Keir. It was kind of you to think of the Milo."

"I hope it helps." He set the mug on the bedside table. "Is there anything else I can do for you, Rowena?"

"Are the children all right?" she asked anxiously.

"Yes. Fast asleep."

"You were good with them today. And tonight." Her big green eyes were darkly soulful. "I appreciate it. Very much."

"It's a pleasure."

"You really mean that, don't you?"

"Yes."

"Keir..." She flashed him a look of vulnerable appeal. "Sit with me?" She shifted somewhat gracelessly, nervously, to make room for him beside her on the bed.

It left him no option but to oblige her request. She would interpret any retreat as rejection. Unfortunately, her movement had pulled the soft fabric of the T-shirt so that her breasts were delineated too clearly for Keir's comfort. He tore his gaze away from them as he lowered himself gingerly on the bed, determined to be the friend she needed.

"Will you hold my hand?" she asked huskily, offering it for him to take.

He shot her a swift, searching look, wondering if she felt frightened and lonely. Her lashes were lowered, her gaze fixed on the inviting hand. Her face had a soft, pearlescent glow in the lamplight. Her lips were slightly apart as though waiting to shape more words. Or perhaps anticipating, wanting the kind of kiss he had given her before starting on his quest.

Keir grimly leashed in that thought. He couldn't afford to give in to temptation when Rowena already had too much to deal with. He turned more towards her so he could enfold her hand in both of his, feeling both tender and possessive **as** his fingers stroked softly over her inner wrist.

Her pulse leapt under his touch. Again he glanced at her, sharply questioning. Her gaze remained fixed on their hands, and she was absolutely still, as though even her breathing was suspended.

What was she thinking? What did his touch mean to her?

"I want you to..." She hesitated, drew in a deep breath. "I want us..." She spoke more strongly, but with a slight quaver that suggested she was screwing up her courage. "To make love."

His heart stopped, then seemed to catapult around his chest with chaotic abandonment of any control whatsoever. Her gaze flew to his, her eyes dark, swirling pools of tortured uncertainties, yet overlaid with a desperate pleading for him to sort them out for her.

No, no, his mind screamed. He wanted it free and clear of anyone else, proving nothing, a joyous celebration of finding each other again, loving because it was beautiful to love. Yet he felt his body stir, urging him to appease the need that had raged in him for so long. She would respond. She had to. Or there was no sense in any of the feelings he'd nursed all these years.

"Tell me it's not because of what Phil Goodman did to you," he heard himself say, his voice uncharacteristically harsh, riven with deep and violent emotions. "If this is some hit back at him, Rowena..."

"No! It's not, Keir."

He saw the recoil in her eyes and both gloried in it and regretted it. Was he spoiling everything? He couldn't help himself. The need to have her all to himself, cleaving only to him, was so powerfully imbedded it reeked of the primitive, but he didn't care. He couldn't be civilised about this. She was his woman, and he didn't want the slightest taint of another man coming between them when they made love.

"I need to know...about us, Keir," she pleaded. Her fingernails scraped the palm of his hand in her agitation at his reaction. Her eyes begged him to understand.

Not another test, he thought in violent rejection. She couldn't turn making love with him into a test. He wouldn't let her. It was too demeaning, too repugnant to him.

He set her hand on the bedclothes and stood up. He couldn't bear her look of hurt. "I have needs, too, Rowena," he stated baldly. He hurt, as well. He hurt all over. He turned aside lest he break and give in to her, even knowing it was wrong and possibly destructive to both of them. He walked away from her because he had to, or nothing would turn out right. Even his bones ached.

"Keir..." Anguish.

He felt it, too. "I hear you, Rowena. I hear your grief and your pain, your doubts and your fears. I understand them all. But I can only give so much." He reached the door he had left ajar and held it to reinforce his resolve to go when he'd said what needed saying.

"Don't you want me?"

The lost little-girl voice pierced his heart and shattered his defences. The passions he had tried so hard to contain exploded through his mind and ripped through his body. "Want you!" The breath hissed from his lungs. He slammed the door shut and wheeled to face her.

"Want you!" he repeated, words jamming in their tumult to be expressed, then spilling into a torrent. "Have you any idea how it felt to be suddenly confronted with you last year, you at Phil Goodman's side, his wife? I didn't even dare ask you to dance with me. It made me sick to watch you with him, wanting...wanting what I couldn't have.''

She stared at him, dumbstruck by his vehemence. At least he had her full attention, Keir thought with fierce satisfaction.

"And I had to work with your husband, knowing he went home to you every night,'' he said, hammering the emotional dilemma *he* had faced. ''I couldn't make myself get rid of him. I'd given him a well-paid executive job. Maybe you needed the money, I reasoned. But the truth, the deep-down basic truth was I didn't want to give up the link to you, Rowena.''

She shook her head, as though dazed by his revelations.

It spurred him to lay it all out for her, so she would understand and realise the length and depth and breadth of what she was asking of him.

''I could hardly believe it when Phil started flirting with Adriana. At first I was angry on your behalf. How could he play around when he had you as his wife? Then as the affair ripened into full-blown infidelity, I took a different attitude.''

He paused, warning signals flashing in his brain. Was he flagellating her with too much honesty?

"What?" she asked.

It was enough to goad him on. ''I wanted your marriage to break up. I wanted him out of your

life so I could step into it. And if that shocks
you, I'm sorry, but it's a measure of my
wanting.''

She said nothing. She simply stared at him.

Too late to retract anything now. He felt too
raw himself to do any healing. ''Then you came
to fight for him.'' He flung the words at her. ''To
fight for a man who cared so little about hurting
you. While I . . . I'd die for you, Rowena.''

Utter stillness from her. Silence.

His hands lifted and fell in a gesture of despair. ''Want you . . .'' The words were a whip to
tortured passion. ''I've wanted you most of my
life. But when we made love all those years ago,
Rowena, you came to me as a woman who wanted
me equally as much, and I will not accept less.
To ask me to make love on the chance that it
might make you feel better about yourself—''

''No, Keir. It wasn't that,'' she swiftly denied.

''Then what? A test of what you feel with
me?''

She didn't answer. Her eyes lost focus as
though she was looking inside herself.

''You want a test?'' he demanded hoarsely.
''I'll give you a test, Rowena.'' He hauled off his
T-shirt and tossed it on the floor. ''I've already
stripped myself naked for you in every other way.
Let's get down to the absolute basics.''

She made no protest as he savagely removed
his other clothes. Then he stood before her, ostensibly at ease, arms akimbo, deliberately challenging her with his nudity, his eyes blazing forth

his need. "You want us to make love?" His voice shook with the force of it. "Then come to me, Rowena. Show me you want me. Not as some panacea for other ills, but wanting me for the man I am."

Her focus was certainly on him now.

The air between them was charged with tension.

Decision time.

She moved. Keir could hardly believe it. Hope tingled through him, electrifying every nerve end. Bedclothes tossed aside, long bare legs reaching for the floor. His heart pounded in his ears. She stood. Her arms crossed, hands bunching folds of the T-shirt. Without hesitation she yanked it over her head and hurled it aside.

Keir's stomach contracted as the full flood of her nakedness hit him, more womanly than he remembered, softer, lushly feminine. His loins tightened, desire shooting through him, vessels expanding, wanting. This was Rowena now, Rowena who had borne him a son in her rounded belly, suckled his baby at her breasts, such glorious breasts, their nipples tightly pointed at him.

There was a magnificent air of pride and confidence in the way she held herself as she walked towards him, shoulders back, hips swaying, her gaze fixed unwaveringly on his, her eyes fiercely aglow. No defeat in her, no grief. Keir exulted in the breaking of those deadly chains, exulted in the freedom with which she came to him.

"I want you, Keir." Her husky voice caressed the last dregs of torment from his mind. "I've always wanted you." Her words burned the scars from his heart. "And that's the naked truth," she said, touching him.

The dark, empty places in his soul exploded in a cascade of light, like brilliant fireworks erupting in showers of stars, wondrous patterns imprinting themselves in renewed bursts, the ecstatic revival of all he had feared lost.

As her hands slid up his chest and linked around his neck, he crushed her body to his, craving the oneness he knew was theirs, unlocked from seemingly impassable doors that had been shut so devastatingly between them. His mouth found hers with a hunger she returned, her passion matching his, her need as wild and as insatiable. The kisses were long and infinitely sweet in their total lack of inhibition.

But they weren't enough. Not nearly enough. His hands swept down the sensual curve of her back, curled around her bottom, cradling the intimate heat of her closer, wanting the ultimate joining, his flesh sheathed in hers, together as they had been, would be.

She stretched on tiptoe, as eager as he for the exquisite sensation of desire fulfilled. "Lift me, Keir," she urged, parting her legs for him, winding them around his hips as he hoisted her higher, ready for the seeking, the finding, the thrust that took him inside her, deep as she settled around him, her muscles convulsing with the pleasure of containing him.

The ecstasy of it, Rowena wanting him as he wanted her. He swung her around in sheer elation, carrying her with him to the bed, smoothly accommodating her position on top of him, inciting the rhythm with hands and thighs, moving to match her, to excite, to thrill to the beat, the slide and the plunge. And her lovely full breasts dangling above him, inviting capture, suction.

The fantastic freedom of drawing her flesh into his mouth, lashing the taut nipple with his tongue, pulling, tugging, the seductive music of her gasps and moans of pleasure as he moved from one breast to the other, taking them in tandem, greedy for the taste of her, for the feel of her response to him, the silky heat of her bathing his pulsing shaft until her shattered cry and the milky flood of her climax spurred him to take the control that had melted for her.

Gently he rolled her onto the pillows where she sank into languid abandonment of any further action. Her thighs were still aquiver. He cradled her hips and pushed to the place that he knew would increase her pleasure. She arched as he reached it, caressed it. An inarticulate cry broke from her throat. Her eyes flew open, and their wonderment filled him with joy as they mirrored the intense inner world he built for them, the soft undulations and the high peaks.

He sustained it as long as he could, but when she lifted her hands and ran her fingertips over his shoulders and chest, his entire body was ignited with excitement and the dance he had orchestrated fell apart to the drumbeat of uncontrollable need. He drove hard and fast, and she lifted herself to give him the fullness of his pleasure, welcoming the ultimate release of his love for her, her arms waiting to receive him as the final melding came.

It was good simply to hold her close in the blissful contentment of knowing all the barriers had been crossed. *Mine at last,* he thought, intensely happy, uncaring of any problems that might arise from what might be viewed as a premature coupling. It wasn't to him. It wasn't to Rowena, either. The wanting had been deep and mutual.

CHAPTER FIFTEEN

ROWENA lay in his arms, incredulity, awe, bliss, drifting across her mind, like shining clouds, pierced by a sun that dispelled all gloom.

Keir.

His name alone embodied a wealth of feeling for Rowena. She had forgotten or suppressed the magic of loving and being loved by him. And to think she had spent eleven years without this brilliant sense of being utterly, poignantly, beautifully alive.

She nestled closer to him, tucking her head under his chin, giving herself more reach to play her hand over Keir's magnificently male body. He hadn't changed at all, not in nature, not in heart, not in any way that counted. He was Keir, her first love, the love that would always endure. She knew that now.

How bravely and passionately he had ripped the scales from her eyes, torn aside the shadows in her mind and smashed the shackles of the eleven long years that had parted them. *My prince, slaying all my dragons,* she thought in smiling whimsy.

"Thank you for being you, Keir," she said with a happy sigh.

"And you . . . you're a miracle, Rowena," he answered softly. "More than I dared dream of."

"I lost faith in dreams," she confessed. "I'm sorry, Keir. I should have trusted you. I should have known. Will you forgive me my blindness?"

He stroked her back, sending delicious little shivers over her skin. "There's nothing to forgive. You had a lot of baggage to carry, Rowena," he said, generously excusing her of any fault.

"I still have," she said, thinking of the children. "You really don't mind about getting a ready-made family?"

"What's yours is mine," he stated simply. "They're great kids. All three of them."

The warmth in his voice left her in no doubt that he accepted them without reservation. And he wouldn't disown any of them. Not like Phil. It wasn't in Keir to renege on commitment.

"Are you worried about them accepting us?" he asked.

Rowena considered the question seriously, then consciously dismissed every niggle of concern. Perhaps she had made the mistake of putting the children's needs first in her marriage to Phil, although certainly not all the time, as Adriana had suggested. What she knew now, with utter conviction, was the love she and Keir shared would always come first. What they had was so special it would rub off on the children, anyway. They could only benefit by it, even if it took some time for it to permeate their lives.

"No, I'm not worried," she replied with firm confidence.

"Good! Then how do you feel about moving in here with me tomorrow?"

She laughed and hitched herself up to see the expression in his eyes. The need and want so clearly emblazoned in their shining depths sobered her. So much time wasted. And who knew how long their lives would be?

"We'll do it," she said decisively.

"You don't mind returning to the house to pack your things?"

She shook her head. Nothing in that house could touch her now. What had been there was gone, irrevocably. Keir was the future, every minute of it.

He grinned. "I'd better give Sarah swimming lessons, too. The sooner they learn, the better. Then you won't have any cause to worry."

He was so generous with everything. "What can I give you, Keir?"

His eyes sparkled with mischief and desire as he rolled her onto her back and leaned over her. "I could suggest many things— " he kissed her, and his voice dropped to a husky throb of contentment "—but the gift of yourself is enough for me, Rowena." He kissed her again, more passionately, thrillingly.

She would think of something to give him, Rowena silently vowed. Something he wasn't expecting. A gift of love that he would know was especially for him, for being the man he was.

CHAPTER SIXTEEN

THE week leading up to Christmas sped by.

There was no protest from the children about moving in to the castle. To Sarah it was a natural progression of the fairy tale. Emily reasoned that Daddy had packed up and left what had been the family home, so it was only right to do the same. Jamie's energy level hit a new high. He could barely contain his excitement at beginning a new life with his real father. Plus a computer to play with.

Keir was marvellous. Both Sarah and Emily learnt to swim very quickly under his patient tuition. He bought video games for the computer, some of which were simple enough for the girls to play, too, although Jamie was put in charge of them and had the responsibility of showing and helping.

The highlight of the week was the Christmas pantomime of *Cinderella*, which was showing in the city. Keir provided them with tickets to a matinee, and the performance was an absolute delight, much talked about afterwards, with the children giving Keir renditions of the parts they loved best. His enjoyment of their mimicking added enormously to their pleasure in the outing.

None of them questioned her sharing a bedroom with Keir. Maybe they accepted it as natural, Rowena thought, given the fact of living together as a family. Maybe they wanted everything to feel natural. She hoped that when Phil came to see the girls on Christmas morning, he wouldn't stir up any uneasy feelings about it.

Keir had informed Phil they had left the house at Killarney Heights and were living with him at Lane Cove. Only personal belongings had been taken with them, so if Phil wished to dispose of the furniture he could do what he liked with it. Rowena and the children would not be returning to the house, which could be put on the market immediately if Phil and Adriana had no use for it.

Phil was also informed that the move in no way affected his right to see his daughters, and both Emily and Sarah had been told of his intention to visit them on Christmas morning. Keir assured Rowena that the conversation had been conducted in a civilised manner, but she could not help having some trepidation about Phil's manner with the girls when he had them to himself.

Keir opened a bank account for her and urged her to spend freely. He wanted this Christmas to be the best ever for all of them. They decorated a marvellous tree in the living room. Rowena had already bought most of her gifts for the children, but she added a few more for extra surprises, and indulged herself in finding some special gifts for Keir.

She laid the festively wrapped parcels out under the tree once she was sure the children were asleep on Christmas Eve. To her astonishment, Keir added a heap of his own, which he'd kept hidden in the boot of his car.

"It's great having kids for Christmas," he told her with a happy grin. "I can't remember when I've had so much fun shopping."

It slid into Rowena's mind that Phil had always left gift shopping for the children to her. Too much hassle with the crowds and too little time to think about it, he had excused himself. She should have known Keir would be different. Thinking about what would give them pleasure was second nature to him. Doing it *was* his pleasure.

As expected, they were woken early on Christmas morning with cries of feverish excitement. Every gift was unwrapped with gleeful anticipation and greeted with delight. Keir had made some inspired choices. Best of all to the children was a three-dimensional jigsaw puzzle of a fantasy castle. The picture of the completed construction showed it had turrets, balconies, open arches, drawbridges and a moat, as well as cobblestoned courtyard gardens with realistic grass, water and rocks. It was, in fact, a detailed model of a classic medieval castle.

One of Keir's gifts to Rowena was the title deed of his house, transferred into her name, making

her the legal owner. On its accompanying
Christmas card he had written, "The security I
want you to have, with all my love, Keir."

Impossible to protest. Rowena wished again
there was something special she could give him,
something of similar value in so far as it would
answer a need he had. She was busy in the
kitchen, preparing the traditional roast turkey,
when Jamie, in response to some question from
Keir, fetched the photograph album devoted to
him. The answer Rowena had been looking for
struck her forcefully as Keir leafed through the
album.

Photos of Jamie as a baby, as a toddler, his
first day at kindergarten. There was a sad, re-
gretful look on Keir's face—years forever lost to
him, joys he hadn't shared. She remembered his
words—*the children I wanted with her.*

A baby, Rowena thought.

She was only twenty-eight. She wouldn't mind
having another baby with Keir, and he would love
it so, sharing intimately the experience of birth
and a new life unfolding. She was privately rev-
elling in the pleasure it would give him when the
door chimes rang.

Phil!

She had been half hoping he wouldn't come at
all, not wanting the day to be soured in any way.
But he was the girls' father, and rights had to be
observed. Emily and Sarah looked up from their
new toys.

"Is that Daddy?" Emily asked.

It had just gone ten-thirty. "I think so," Rowena answered, giving them an encouraging smile to put them at ease. "Shall we go and see?"

"Well, I'm going to play my new computer game," Jamie announced, proudly independent of Phil. "Want to have a look with me, Keir?"

"Yes. It should be quite a challenge for you, Jamie," he obliged, moving to give his son the reassurance he needed.

It felt wrong to have the family separated like this, but there was nothing that could be done about it. Rowena gathered up the girls, who had gone oddly quiet, looking after Jamie and Keir as they walked along the gallery to the study and not expressing any excitement whatsoever over the visit by their father. Nevertheless, they compliantly followed Rowena to the front door and didn't hang back when she opened it.

One step onto the porch and all three of them came to a dead halt.

Phil was accompanied by Adriana Leigh.

Neither of them looked as though they had come to entertain two little girls. Phil was in a smart navy blue suit and Adriana was semi-clothed in a red and gold sundress that showed plenty of cleavage and leg. Rowena and the girls were wearing jeans and T-shirts printed with bright Christmas motifs. The contrast in dress instantly created a distance between the two parties.

"Well, how are my girls?" Phil began with forced heartiness, not bothering with Christmas greetings to Rowena.

"Who is *she*?" Sarah demanded, eyeing Adriana up and down with hostile suspicion.

"Don't be rude, Sarah," Rowena softly reproved. "Your father will introduce you."

"This is my friend Adriana. We're going to take you and Emily to a big park where you can play on the swings and the slippery dip," Phil said unctuously.

While they sat and twiddled their thumbs until time was up, Rowena thought. Adriana's high heels were definitely not park shoes. Which raised the question of how much supervision the children would get.

Sarah gave Adriana a baleful stare and bluntly stated her decision. "I'm not going anywhere with the wicked witch!"

"What?" Phil snapped.

Rowena barely stopped herself from rolling her eyes.

"She'll put a spell on me," Sarah explained. "I'm going back inside the castle. She can't get me there because the prince won't let her."

Before anyone could stop her she turned tail and ran into the foyer, heading full pelt towards the gallery.

"What the hell is this, Rowena?" Phil demanded testily. "Have you been bad-mouthing Adriana to my daughters?"

"No, I haven't. Sarah has her own way of working things out, Phil. You know she does," she pleaded in mitigation.

"You could have corrected her," he accused.

"I tried." Though not very hard, she had to admit to herself. After all, she couldn't see why she should defend Adriana in the circumstances. The woman was not interested in children, and that was as obvious as the dress she wore.

"I didn't think you'd be spiteful," Phil said, sniping.

Rowena held her tongue, wondering how he described his actions to himself.

He gave up badgering her and dropped to his haunches to court Emily. "How's Daddy's girl? Have you missed me?"

Emily shrank back against Rowena. "Why did you leave us, Daddy?" she bravely asked.

Phil sighed. "Well, it's hard to explain. I wasn't really happy with your mother, Emily."

"Don't you love Mummy any more?"

"I'm much happier with Adriana," he stated firmly. "That's why I'm with her. And you'll like her very much once you get to know her."

Emily looked at Adriana, who obliged with an indulgent smile, which was enough to turn Rowena's stomach. Emily wasn't much taken with it, either. She returned her gaze to her father and continued her childish inquisition.

"What about me, Daddy? Weren't you happy with me?"

"Emily..." Phil flushed uncomfortably. "When you're grown up, you need to be with another grown-up. That doesn't mean I don't love my little girl. I've got lots of Christmas presents in the car for you."

"Have you got Mummy's lamp for her? The one with the blue beads hanging down?"

"No, I haven't," he growled. "Now let's get going. We haven't got all day." He straightened up and offered his hand to her.

Emily looked doubtfully at Adriana, then shook her head, her hand seeking Rowena's, not Phil's. "I want to stay with Mummy."

"Emily, I've come out of my way to see you," Phil said tersely. "Your mother said you wanted me to."

"Yes." She nodded gravely. "Thank you for seeing me, Daddy, but I don't want to go with you," she said in a very little voice.

"All right," Phil snapped. "If that's the way you want it, I'll give all your presents to the Smith family."

"Phil," Rowena reproved quickly. "You can't force things. It would have been wiser to come without Adriana this time."

"You can say that when you're living openly with Keir Delahunty?" he scoffed.

Keir appeared in the doorway, Sarah's hand firmly clasped in his, Jamie on his other side. "Is there a problem?" he asked, politely nodding to Phil and Adriana.

"No. No problem," Phil mocked. "I only came to do my duty, and that's done. Have yourself a happy family Christmas." He stepped smartly back to Adriana and took her arm. "Come on, darling. We've spent enough time here."

"Happy Christmas!" Adriana trilled, delighted to have the duty disposed of.

Keir stepped out to stand at Rowena's side. Jamie came forward to put his arm around Emily's shoulders in big-brotherly support. They all watched Phil and Adriana get into what had to be Adriana's car, since it wasn't the red Mazda convertible.

"He said he'd give our presents away, Sarah," Emily said mournfully.

"I don't want them anyway," Sarah declared unequivocally. "I bet the wicked witch touched them."

She was undoubtedly right, Rowena thought. Phil would have got Adriana to buy them for him. She had the feeling it would be a long time before Phil came visiting again.

"He didn't bring Mummy her lamp, either," Emily added, clearly affected by the injustice of it all.

The car zoomed away from the kerb and disappeared down the street.

"We've got the prince, Emily," Sarah said, her satisfaction in the choice abundantly clear.

"Yes. We've got the prince," Emily agreed with fervour.

Jamie gave Keir a smug look. "And we've got lots of presents inside," he reminded the girls.

"Yes!" they shouted in unison.

"Let's play!" It was like a bugle call.

"Yes!"

Jamie led the charge into the house, the girls on his heels, the encounter with Phil shrugged off and left behind them with what seemed like extraordinary ease. Emily, at Jamie's urging, ran with him to the study to see what was on the computer screen, and Sarah skipped down the gallery, as carefree as an impish little fairy.

Keir closed the front door and drew Rowena into a gentle embrace, his dark velvet eyes scanning hers for stress. "Are you all right?" he asked. "Phil didn't upset you?"

"No." She released her inner tension with a sigh, then smiled her relief at the unexpected outcome of Phil's visit. "Children can be so amazing."

"Their logic is very direct," he said dryly.

"Keir..." She wound her arms around his neck and pressed closer. Her eyes projected all the desire in her heart, desire for him, desire to please, to give, to share all life had to offer. "Let's have another baby. Together."

Surprise and delight lit his eyes. "You mean it, Rowena? You really want another child?"

She laughed, her heart lifting exultantly at his response. "Well, we needn't stop at one if you want more," she teased. "I'm pretty good at being a mother, you know."

"The best." He grinned. "I'd love a big family, Rowena. Having been an only child..."

Of course! That was why he and Brett had been inseparable—the only child in each family until she had come along, the much-loved little sister.

"But what about you?" He quickly changed tack. "I thought you might like to pick up the arts course you'd wanted to do."

"I can do that in my thirties. Or my forties. I'm planning on a long life."

He laughed, his eyes shining with unadulterated happiness. "A very long and a very full life."

"How could it be anything else with you?"

"And with you."

Their lips met in a kiss that sealed so many things—the love and the giving and the open trust and the sense of completely bonded togetherness.

A new start.

CHAPTER SEVENTEEN

FAY PENDLETON, Keir's wonderful all-purpose secretary, bustled around them in the nave of the church, making sure the bridal procession was arranged to proceed perfectly.

Jamie was in the lead, dressed in a formal black pageboy suit, carrying a white satin cushion on which lay the two gold wedding rings.

Emily came next, then Sarah, both looking absolutely exquisite in flower-girl gowns of ivory raw silk. Seed pearls enhanced the lace on their bodices and outlined the waistline. Frills and bows ornamented softly puffed sleeves, and the full skirts were caught at the back with a feature bow. Around their hair were circlets of little pink florabunda roses and baby's breath, and they carried beautifully decorated baskets of rose petals to sprinkle down the aisle.

"There! Now don't twitch or anything," Fay advised Rowena. "I've got the train just right. You're ready to go. I'll signal the organist before taking my seat."

Rowena smiled. "Thank you for organising everything for me, Fay. You've been marvellous."

"It's been a real pleasure, Rowena. Like having a daughter."

She moved to the head of the aisle and gave them one last look-over, nodded approval, then set off for her seat at the front of the church. It would be easy for the organist to spot her, Rowena thought. Fay had her hair dyed a fiery copper and was wearing a vibrant violet outfit.

Sarah disobeyed the eyes-forward edict and turned her head to catch one more admiring eyeful of her transformed mother. "You look just like a princess, Mummy," she whispered, a note of awe in her voice.

"Thank you, Sarah," Rowena whispered back, her heart swelling with happiness.

She *felt* like a princess. Keir had insisted they be married in a traditional fairy-tale wedding, and she was to buy the dress of her dreams, no expense spared. When she had seen this wedding gown she had just stared and stared at it, spellbound, finding it utterly magical and perfect in every detail.

It was made of ivory silk duchess satin and had an air of elegant majesty about it. The empire sleeves, cinched waist and deep neckline evoked a bygone era. The wide flare of the skirt created a wonderful balance to the tightly fitted bodice. It featured a centre gore encrusted with lace and pearls, repeating the pattern sewn onto the flared lower half of the sleeves.

In keeping with the style of the dress, the veil was attached to a tiara of fine gold and tiny ivory flowers. Rowena's hair had been swept up into a high topknot, which the tiara encircled. Around her neck she wore a fine gold chain supporting a beautiful gold and pearl-encrusted cross.

Keir hadn't seen any of it. She hoped—no, she knew—she was everything he wanted in a bride. To him, she would look beautiful whatever she wore, and part of feeling like a princess was knowing her prince was at the altar, waiting for her.

The soft organ playing stopped. There was a hushed expectancy in the church. The "Wedding March" started. Jamie set off down the aisle, keeping in perfect time with the music. Emily correctly paced her entrance, gently scattering rose petals from her basket. Sarah followed on cue, apparently deciding a shower of rose petals was more appropriate. Or more fun.

Rowena couldn't help smiling. She smiled all the way down the aisle—to the friends she had met and made over the past sixteen months while living with Keir, to Aunty Bet and her son and his family, who had flown down from Queensland for the wedding, to Keir's parents, who were so delighted to be getting Rowena as their daughter-in-law, and finally to the man she loved and always would love.

Keir.

He looked stunningly handsome in black, peak-lapel tails and white wing-collar shirt, so elegant and debonair. The classic style gave him such a distinguished air. But it was the expression in his eyes that mattered most to

Rowena, the shining of a love that had spanned so many years without ever faltering.

She wished her parents could have been here, not as they were after Brett's death, but before, when they had been happy to have Keir as almost a second son, happy for her to go out with him. She hoped they had found peace and perhaps were even looking down at her and Keir right now, knowing it was right for them to have come together again.

The marriage service began.

She thought fleetingly of her marriage to Phil, wondering if he was as happy as he wanted to be with Adriana. He had resigned from Delahunty's over a year ago, investing the money from the sale of the house in a real estate business on the Gold Coast of Queensland. The fast-paced life there suited them better, he had said, and the girls could come and have a vacation with him when they were old enough to travel alone.

Their parting was reasonably amicable. So was their divorce. There was no question over the custody of the children, and formal visiting rights were waived. The girls could contact him if they wanted to, but basically he had simply dropped out of their lives, and Rowena didn't believe he was missed.

Keir more than filled the gap.

Keir.

Their commitment to each other was at last being formalised in this marriage service, husband and wife in the eyes of the world, yet the inner bonding went back a long, long way and would go on forever. Rowena was certain of that. No doubts. No fears. The rapture in her heart was completely unshadowed.

Keir slid the gold ring on her finger. She slid the matching ring on his. They said the words that sealed the promise of togetherness. They kissed. They signed the marriage certificate. They were one.

Then Keir's parents came forward, his mother lovingly laying Keir's and Rowena's new baby son in Rowena's arms. He was clothed in the same beautiful ivory christening robes Keir had worn thirty-six years ago. They moved over to the christening font. Fay Pendleton proudly joined them as designated godmother. Aunty Bet's son, Darren, who was godfather to Jamie, stepped up to take on the same responsibility for Jamie's new brother. The children clustered around to complete the family grouping.

Brett Keir Delahunty.

To Rowena the name symbolised so much that was good—friendship, trust, sharing and caring.

Once the christening ceremony was over, Jamie declared he had something to say, and he and Emily and Sarah had agreed that this was the time to say it. The girls nodded vigorously. Keir smiled at his older son, his eyes shining with love and pride.

"Say what's on your mind, Jamie," he invited, happily confident it would not be amiss.

"It's like this," Jamie started, then turned to address Rowena. "When Brett gets a bit older and begins learning words, he'll be saying Dada when he sees Keir, won't he, Mum?"

Rowena hadn't thought that far. "It would be the natural thing, Jamie," she answered, feeling strongly that Keir shouldn't be deprived of the joy of hearing Dada for the first time.

"And he's our brother," Jamie went on, "so he might get confused if we don't call Keir Dad. We're all in the same family."

His reasoning was wonderfully clear, beautifully clear. A brilliant smile burst from Rowena's heart. "That's true, Jamie," she encouraged.

He looked at Keir. "So if it's okay with you, Emily and Sarah and I would like to call you Dad from now on."

Emily and Sarah lifted brightly expectant faces to him.

"I'd like that very much," Keir assured them all, his voice deepening with emotion, a sheen of tears making his eyes even shinier.

"I'd rather call you Daddy," Emily appealed.

"Daddy is fine, Emily. Whatever you're comfortable with," Keir said warmly.

She beamed.

Rowena's heart turned over. Such full acceptance from Emily meant she really felt she belonged to Keir.

"I like Dada," Sarah declared. "Dada, Dada, Dada," she trilled with uninhibited glee. "Brett will learn real fast from me, Dada."

Keir laughed. "I'm sure he will, Sarah."

And he'll live in a fairy-tale wonderland with Sarah as his guide, Rowena thought. Her younger daughter was utterly entranced with the baby, and her attachment to Keir had never been in question. He had entered her life as the prince, and Rowena suspected that when Sarah grew up, there would be many a man who'd find himself being measured against the prince, and woe betide them if they didn't reach the mark.

"That's it, Dad," Jamie said with a huge grin. "We can move out now."

Keir returned the grin, father to son. "Lead the way, Jamie."

Rowena passed baby Brett to Keir and curled her arm around his for the long walk down the aisle and out of the church. Their eyes caught in a magic moment of love, utterly fulfilled.

His wife, Keir thought, his heart so full it was fit to burst. He looked down at the baby cradled in his other arm. *His son.* He watched Emily and Sarah take their places in the procession behind Jamie. *His family.*

To be so blessed ... the wonder and glory of it.

Their wedding day.